Evangelina Takes Flight

Diana J. Noble

PIÑATA
BOOKS

PIÑATA BOOK
ARTE PÚBLICO PI
HOUSTON, TEXA

Evangelina Takes Flight is funded in part by grants from the City of Houston through the Houston Arts Alliance and the Texas Commission on the Arts. We are grateful for their support.

Piñata Books are full of surprises!

Arte Público Press
University of Houston
4902 Gulf Fwy, Bldg 19, Rm 100
Houston, Texas 77204-2004

Cover design by Victoria Castillo
Photo by Stephanie Rengel

Cataloging-in-Publication (CIP) Data for *Evangelina Takes Flight* is available.

Printed in the United States of America
May 2017–June 2017
Cushing-Malloy, Inc., Ann Arbor, MI
7 6 5 4 3 2 1

Dedication

To Russ, Taylor (x2), Adam and Sierra who fill me with inspiration, strength and purpose.

Acknowledgements

For someone who once thought, "I'm no good at creative writing," and "I don't have enough ideas to dream up an entire story worth reading," it's a wonder I ever got past myself enough to write this book. If it weren't for a special group of family and friends, I wouldn't have made it across the finish line.

First and foremost I must thank my parents, Belinda and Arturo who've always been models of integrity, and instilled in me the love of family and pride in our rich cultural heritage. Dad, special thanks to you for the countless hours you invested as my idea generator, history buff, cheerleader, researcher and proof reader. Thanks also to friends Anne Frantilla, Helen Carlson, Sandy Barnes and Cindy Flegenheimer for their honest opinions, wise counsel and endless support. And finally, to my grandmothers, Adelfa Garcia Jacobs and Evangelina Escobar Zárate for being the loving, resilient role models and matriarchs who started it all.

PART 1

Chapter One
The Coming Storm

May 19, 1911, Rancho Encantado (Enchanted Ranch) outside Mariposa, a small town in northern Mexico

Papá thought I didn't hear him talking to my brother, but I did, because I pressed my ear against the cracks in the barn wall, and now his hushed "Don't-tell-anyone-about-this" voice thunders in my head.

"We're landowners, *m'ijo*. If they do come here, they'll show us no mercy."

I grip the fencepost outside the chicken pen and command my legs to stop wobbling. He did say *if*.

I make my way to the kitchen on the backside of the house, my front apron pocket bulging with warm eggs.

Mamá stands behind the massive carved wood table dotted with woven baskets full of peppers, garlic, cilantro and limes. With nine of us to feed, she's either behind that table, at the sink or in front of the stove most of the day.

"I have to tell you something," I announce as I unload the eggs into the rust-colored clay bowl.

She puts down her knife and wipes her hands on the front of her apron. "Of course, *m'ija*, what is it?"

3

"The soldiers are coming," the words spill out. "What's going to happen to us?" I open and clench my clammy palms.

Mamá sighs and steps toward me with outstretched arms, her expression a familiar mix of love, pity and exasperation. "Where did you hear that, *m'ija?*" Her arms fold around me. The warmth of her body melts into mine.

"Outside," I whisper into her shoulder. "Papá was talking to Emilio. I was feeding the chickens."

She pushes me back and studies my face. "So you were listening to someone else's conversation?"

"I wasn't trying to," I respond as I gnaw on the nail of my little finger. "Well, maybe I was. But, that's not important! Should we leave Mariposa?"

"Evangelina . . . " Mamá shakes her head. "Your father will let us know if there's any reason for worry. Right now we have a *quinceañera* to put on. In the next week, I'm going to need your help more than ever. All right? And, *m'ija?*" She purses her lips. "Stop it with the nails, such a dirty habit." She guides my hand away from my mouth.

"Yes, Mamá," I say dutifully through clenched teeth. She didn't give me any answers at all. "I'll go see if Elsa is up," I mutter and shuffle toward the bedroom I share with my sister.

"Evangelina?" Mamá calls from down the hall.

"Yes?"

"Do not say anything to your brothers or sisters about this."

"Why not?"

"Just do as I say."

"*Claro que sí.*" I swallow, but the lump in my dry throat sits like a rock in still water.

"Do I have your word?"

I close the bedroom door as if I didn't hear the question. Elsa, my almost-fifteen-year-old sister, primps in front of the mirror at the dressing table. She pulls a hairpin from her pocket and pushes it in the long black braid piled neatly on top of her head in a perfect bun.

"Good morning, Evangelina! Did you get the eggs?" A perfect curl hangs in front of each ear.

"Of course, I got up an hour ago, hauled water from the river, fed the chickens *and* got the eggs while you were snoring away."

She looks at me, aghast. "I don't snore!"

"How would you know if you're asleep?"

"Mamá is going to make bread pudding, for the *quinceañera*." She ignores my question, turning back to the mirror. "We're going to need a lot of eggs."

I wrinkle my nose. "That's a Christmas dessert."

"I know, but it's my favorite, and Enrique's, too."

A *quinceañera* is more than a girl's fifteenth birthday celebration; it's an announcement to the world that she's eligible for marriage. Elsa and Enrique turn fifteen on May twenty-eight. My own *quinceañera* is less than a year and a half away.

"I'm worried," I whisper. I plop down on the edge of our bed.

Elsa turns in the chair to face me and folds her hands in her lap. "And?"

"Mamá said not to tell anyone, but I just have to or I'll burst."

She throws up her hands. "Don't be so dramatic. Are you sure you should tell me?"

I shake my head. "No."

She bites her lip for a moment. "Oh, just tell me! I don't want you to burst!"

I lean forward. "I was outside this morning, early, while you were in here snoring." I throw that in again just because. "I fed the chickens like I always do. A few pecked at the feed, but most of them ran around all nervous."

"Evangelina, how do you know if a chicken is nervous?" She folds a handkerchief and places it in her apron pocket.

"They wouldn't eat. They just ran around flapping and pecking at each other."

"They're chickens. Does it matter?"

"A storm is coming. They can sense it."

"Evangelina, is that what you wanted to tell me? The chickens seeing a storm in our future?"

"Don't be ridiculous. I'm not just talking about rain and wind. Something bad is going to happen." I lower my voice. "Papá talked to the sheriff in Castillo yesterday, and this morning he told Emilio something—a warning from the sheriff." I take a deep breath. "The revolution is coming this way."

"What do you mean?"

"Have you heard of Pancho Villa?"

"Of course. Everyone's heard of him. He takes from the rich and gives to the poor, like Robin Hood."

"No!" I shake my head. "Well, maybe." I press the heel of my palm on the space between my eyebrows. "Maybe he *was* a hero, but now his troops are burning houses, stealing and . . . and worse." Papá said what "worse" is, but I keep it to myself.

Elsa grabs my hands and squeezes. "But the revolution's at the other end of the country."

"The sheriff said a battle broke out in Los Palos last week. The town was practically destroyed."

"What should we do?" Her face turns as pale as a cotton blossom.

"I don't know."

"What did Papá say after that?"

"Nothing. He and Emilio walked away." I stand up and look through the window. A see-through curtain of mist floats down and turns into a steady rain. Thunder rolls in the distance. A storm is definitely coming.

"Do you think we'll still have the *quinceañera*?"

"Mamá said there's a lot to do before then, so that must be a 'yes.' Let's just do our chores and try to forget all about this. It was selfish of me to say anything to you," I concede. I only told her to make myself feel better. "Please, please, don't tell Mamá I said anything."

Chapter Two
What Will Happen, Will Happen

May 21, 1911

Mamá serves *papas con huevo,* eggs scrambled with potatoes and flour tortillas for dinner. I rolled out the tortillas myself, but instead of round, they came out looking like South America, Australia and a square.

"Square, triangle, circle . . . they all taste the same," Abuelito, my grandfather, always says.

My hollow stomach aches, but I only eat a few bites. Mamá and Elsa clear the dishes, and I wash and dry by myself. It's just as well. I don't feel like talking. The dishrag swishes back and forth through the warm water. Dishes clink and clatter. I dry the last plate and set it on top of the others in the cupboard. Why put dishes away when they'll be pulled out at least two more times and put back again, only to start all over again the next morning?

I asked Abuelito this question once.

"*M'ija,* if you followed that logic you'd never wipe your own behind. Why wipe when you know it's going to get *caca* all over it again?" More Abuelito wisdom that leaves no room for argument.

I hang the dishtowel and washrag on the warm stove to dry out, walk to the living room and peer out the front window. Emilio and Enrique help Papá replace rotted boards on the barn. Elsa hangs the last of the wash on the clothesline strung between the twisted hundred-year-old avocado tree and the fig tree, loaded with figs, almost ready for harvest. Not that I haven't already eaten some. Some every day, that is.

Mamá reads the Bible to Tomás and Domingo on the back porch. She and Papá are excellent readers. Both had tutors growing up. Papá's even lived here at the rancho. Our tutor, Profesor Zárate moved back to Mexico City to help Francisco I. Madero win the presidential election, only to have the dictator Porfirio Díaz throw Madero into prison.

I step outside and breathe in deeply. This is the only place I've ever lived. I was born in my parents' bedroom, and so was Papá and two generations before him. A girl from church saw a picture of the Eiffel Tower in a magazine. Now she wants to live in Paris, because Mariposa is "unsophisticated and dull." What's wrong with dull?

I wander into the open field. Paris may have the Eiffel Tower, but it's prettier here when the sun sits just above the horizon. Streaks of orange, red and purple paint the hazy sky. A bright yellow bird with a head as black as coal glides by and settles in a tree with buds that hang like fluffy yellow tassels. Creamy-colored sandstone bricks form the sturdy walls of our home. A wide, worn porch wraps around the house from front to back. Mamá and Papá sit there most evenings and talk until the mosquitoes force them inside. My sisters and I take turns sitting on the wooden-planked floor, cross-legged, while Mamá brushes our hair or braids it for church.

Once or twice a week Abuelito sits in a chair, and we gather around his feet while he tells us about Gorgonio, a brave boy who encounters many improbable adventures. One time, Gorgonio wandered into the woods and stumbled across jewels buried by a Spanish king. Another time Gorgonio got lost in the mountains and gave up hope only to find a talking bear that showed him the way to safety. Every tale is a different adventure, and each one has a unique lesson, mostly having to do with obeying your parents' rules. Abuelito lectures a lot, but at least he tries to make it interesting.

The flowering citrus trees announce their presence each spring with the sweetest, most inviting fragrances. At harvest time we pick the fruit from dawn until dusk. We grow vegetables, too. Corn, tomatoes, squash, onions, beans. Mamá cooks with some, sells some and gives away even more.

I make my way to the tomato plants and pick as many as will fit in my apron folded up into a make-shift sling. Clouds of dirt surround my feet as I come toward the house. Mamá shakes out a kitchen rug up ahead. What should I say to her? That I'm still worried, have been chewing my nails and told Elsa what I wasn't supposed to tell?

"I brought some tomatoes" is all I can think of.

Mamá drops the rug into the basket at her feet and pulls me in tight. Her cinnamon-scented long brown hair brushes against my cheek.

"You were awfully quiet at dinner tonight, and then you disappeared. Is everything all right?"

"Of course. I just took a little walk. There were plenty of ripe tomatoes, and there'll be more in a few days."

"Don't tell me you just wanted to pick tomatoes," she scolds. "Worrying will not change things. What will happen, will happen, and we'll handle it together. It's getting late, so you should go in. I'll be out here for a little bit. Sleep tight, and don't forget to say your prayers."

"*Buenas noches,* Mamá." I blow her a kiss.

Inside I help Elsa get Tomás and Domingo into their pajamas and tuck them in bed. Back in our bedroom I lie down, touch the gold cross I wear around my neck, say my prayers and pull the blanket over my body, head and all. My restless mind, stuck in that murky place between awake and asleep wanders as the daylight gives way to night.

I dream that I'm coming back from the river with a bucket of water, when something in the distance catches my eye—a black-tailed hare scampers across the brush. I can see the terror in its yellow eyes as a large, magnificent hawk closes in and carries it away. It doesn't stand a chance, and there's nothing I can do to stop it.

Chapter Three
Predictable

May 22, 1911

I love my home, my family, our church, even my chores. Most days I know what to do, when to do it and what comes next. Wake up, feed the animals, haul water from the river, mend clothes, wash and dry dishes, shuck and grind corn, make un-round tortillas, watch after my little brothers, tell them nighttime stories and go to bed. It's all so predictable, and that's exactly what I like about it.

It is nine o'clock, and the sun shines through the front windows. *Pan de dulce* bakes in the wood stove. Today's batch is my favorite, *marranitos*, traditional molasses sweetbread cut in the shape of palm-size pigs. I load more wood into the stove and walk to the back porch, where I shuck corn piled high in a wooden crate then grind it for tomorrow's tortillas.

Here, everyone has a role. Francisca, the eldest at nineteen, married René a year and a half ago, a week before her eighteenth birthday. René worked in our orchard for years, still does.

Seventeen-year-old Emilio works as a carpenter when he can get the work. He's Papá's biggest helper on the *rancho*—strong, always willing to help and knows exactly what and when things need to be done.

Elsa does mostly inside chores like me, but takes care of Domingo and Tomás more than I do, although we both do that more since Francisca moved out. Elsa has a crush on a boy she met at church but won't admit it. She's so beautiful with her long glossy black hair and gold-flecked eyes. Boys stare at her, but she pretends not to notice. People say we look similar, but she's the prettier one.

Enrique wants to run the ranch when Papá is too old to do it anymore, which is hard to believe, because he avoids work like a cat avoids water. He picks on me every chance he gets. I'm the smallest girl at church for my age. When kids tease me, Enrique joins in! I've learned to ignore it, or try to ignore it. Okay, I admit. It's hard to ignore.

Last week, five-year-old Tomás jumped off a bed and flapped like a hawk. He hit his forehead on Mamá's sewing box and still has the nasty bruise to show for it. Tomás and trouble go together like coffee and cream, and those things really do go together. Who wants to drink black coffee anyway? Blech!

Four-year-old Domingo is sweet as a summer peach, but he makes my brain tired with all his questions.

Today, Mamá and I cook catfish with lemon, tomato and garlic for lunch. After that, I read to Domingo and get him down for a nap, although I don't think he's going to take naps too much longer. He only pretends to sleep and gets up after half an hour.

Mamá and Tomás head to the orchard to see if any of the late harvest pumpkins held up well enough to make *empanadas*.

Papá and the boys walk back to the farthest edges of the ranch to chop wood and bundle it up to sell. The extra money helps, especially if our crops don't fare well, or even if just one of them does poorly. Last year was a bad year for all our citrus, so Papá and Emilio took extra jobs in town. It took the rest of us to tend the cattle. We fed them, weaned calves from their mothers, moved the herd from pasture to pasture, leveled and seeded the ground and checked the fences to be sure no animals could escape and no coyotes, wolves or bobcats could get in.

Dark has set in, and the crickets chirp their same old song outside my window. I lie in bed, but the pillow feels lumpy, my back aches and I'm too warm.

Like Mexican snow, sleep won't come. I can think better outside with the fresh air, so I walk out onto the front porch. I lower myself into the rocking chair, close my eyes and picture Mamá rocking Domingo to sleep with the movement of the chair's soft rise and fall and her hushed, velvety lullabies.

The porch steps creak.

"Evangelina, what are you doing out here this late at night?" Papá walks toward me in the muddled moonlight, still in his jeans, boots and dirty work shirt. "It's not safe. Señor Treviño found a half-eaten calf in his field just the other morning. Wolves got her. A young girl is not so different from a calf in the eyes of a hungry predator like that."

"I couldn't sleep."

"What is it, *m'ijita*?" Papá kneels down and brings his face closer to mine. His brow knits together and forms two lines between his deep brown eyes.

"The revolution. What happens if the soldiers come here? Will they hurt us? Will they kidnap Emilio and Enrique?"

Papá lifts my chin with the tips of his fingers. "Your mother told me you knew about my conversation with your brother. Well, little Miss Big-Ears," he pretend frowns, "I cannot predict the future. I leave that to God. But I will do everything in my power to keep this family safe."

I stand up and lay my head against his chest. A warm breeze rustles the folds of my nightgown, and the tightness in my chest eases.

Papá walks me back to bed. "Good night *m'ijita*. You'll feel better after some rest."

I climb under the care-worn patchwork quilt Abuelita, my father's mother, made for my third birthday. She died when I was seven. I close my eyes and imagine the nighttime sky—so beautiful, like a blanket of sparkles that covers me and keeps me safe. My fourteenth birthday is just over a month away. I wonder where I will be the morning of July first. No matter what Papá says, I'm convinced it won't be here.

Chapter Four
Tomás

May 24, 1911

I wake to the sound of someone splitting wood out-side and the smell of something delicious. The sun blares through the window, my eyes unable to open more than a sliver. I'm usually the first one out of bed. Dawn is my favorite time of day. Most mornings I go outside, sit on the front porch and feel the heat trickle in, thankful for the time I have to be alone with my thoughts before morning chores. Other days I walk to the river and dip my feet in or throw rocks at the water. Rock throwing is behavior unbecoming of a proper young lady, but at sun-rise, it's just God and me, and He doesn't mind. I know this because He often graces me with a gift of yellows, reds, purples and grays painted across the sky and bright beams of light shooting through the branches of the mesquite trees. The birds flit around dipping their tiny feet in the waters of the Río Bravo, chatting with each other and flying carelessly to and fro. If God didn't want me to throw rocks in the water, He'd send rain instead.

The house is alive outside my doorway. Pans clank, Domingo calls for Mamá, the screen door bangs. I weigh my options. If I go back to sleep, I won't have to think about unpleasant things that make my stomach flip over. Despite my best effort, I just can't sleep, so I toss off the covers and get up.

Mamá stands in the doorway. "Evangelina, Papá needs help outside. Get dressed and take Tomás with you. Just because you slept in doesn't mean you have fewer chores."

"Of course. It's just that I didn't sleep very well." She raises an eyebrow. "I'll finish my chores after dinner. I promise."

She walks away and calls back over her shoulder, "There are a few *empanadas* left in the kitchen. Make sure to eat something before you get started, and don't forget to take Tomás."

The tantalizing fragrance of apples and fresh ground cinnamon fills my nose. The pumpkins were over ripe, so Mamá made my next favorite filling for the *empanadas*. Eager for the flaky little turnovers filled with gooey fruit, I throw on a white cotton dress, slip on my sandals and twist my thick hair into a quick braid. I put on my apron with the big pockets in front and step into the kitchen. Tomás sits at the table, his fingers and face covered in apple mess. He wipes his hands on his pants, turns around and sweeps the room with a guilty-looking glance.

"Tomás," I say sternly. "What are you up to, young man?"

His cheeks flush a watermelon color.

"I'm sorry, Evangelina."

His remorse doesn't last long. A mischievous grin slowly appears. He holds up his left hand, spreads his fingers and licks them one by one.

A small laugh escapes before I can stop it. "Go clean up. Papá needs our help. It's hot outside, so bring your sombrero, or you'll get burned for sure."

I walk to the sink, wet the corner of a small towel and hand it to him.

"Can I have another *empanada*?" He bats his long, swoopy eyelashes.

"It looks like you had more than your share from what I can tell. How many did you eat?"

"Two I think?" His head bows low.

"That's quite enough. Lucky for me there's one left."

Heat waves ripple and float above the parched ground. Papá stands behind the stable and chops wood into pieces short enough to fit in our stove. Without wood we can't cook. If we don't want to eat more than fruits and vegetables, Papá and my brothers chop. Mamá cooks from dawn until dusk—tortillas, beans, chicken with squash, tomatoes and corn, and when we're lucky, rice pudding, my favorite.

Papá swings the axe with such force it splits each piece of wood with one cut. The muscles in his arms shift and slide as he heaves the axe up and down. He lifts his sombrero and uses his handkerchief to wipe the sweat from his forehead and the back of his neck under a thicket of dark curls. He turns to stuff the handkerchief in his back pocket, sees us and waves.

"Well, hello, my little morning glories! I'm sure you came out here, anxious to help me, right?"

Tomás shakes his head and grimaces.

"I need you and Tomás to gather kindling," he says to me. He bends over and gives Tomás a little squeeze. "*Buenos días, m'ijo!* Did you enjoy your *empanadas*?"

"*Sí*, Papá," Tomás says and turns to me. "Evangelina, I have a good idea. You look for wood, and I'll look for a lizard with the spikes on its back. The spikes are soft, you know, and you can push them over with your finger, and it doesn't even hurt them!" He holds up his palms and lifts his shoulders. "Isn't that terrific?"

"I couldn't agree more," I answer. "I need to talk to Papá first, though. You go on, and I'll follow you. Don't climb any trees or go anywhere near the river, you hear?" I kiss him on the cheek, and he skips away.

"Did you tell Mamá what we talked about last night?" I whisper to Papá.

"Your mother and I don't keep secrets from each other. I told her next time I'm in town, I will ask around and let you both know what I find out. In the meantime, go about your day as if nothing's changed, because the truth is, at least for now, nothing has changed. This should be a happy time for all of us. Just think, your own *quinceañera* is not that far off. Before you know it, you and your mother will start talking about your own fiesta! Now go find Tomás. There's a basket inside the stable by the first stall. Fill it with as much kindling as you can. You'll need to make a few trips. And make sure Tomás actually gathers wood. If you don't watch him, he'll spend the whole time seeing how far he can spit! That's a new hobby Enrique taught him."

"Wonderful. I'll have to thank Enrique later." I roll my eyes.

I squeeze Papá tight, then walk into the stable and scan the ground for a horned toad lizard. Maybe I can find one for Tomás so he can give up the search and help me gather wood.

No lizards in here, just a horse, two mules and a skinny, undersized thirteen-year-old who wishes she was stronger, prettier, taller and braver. I kick the hay with each step, pick up the basket, throw the straps over my shoulders and hurry down the road, the empty basket thumping against my back.

It's never a good idea to leave Tomás alone for long. Most five-year-olds have a curious nature, but Tomás makes other kids his age seem disinterested by comparison. A year ago he pushed a bean up his nose so far that no one knew it was there until it sprouted. Doctor Gonzales had quite a time getting it out!

Last week Tomás piled dirt complete with an ant colony into a metal tub. He gave the little critters bits of leftover tortilla and watched them scurry along with their treasure, tirelessly building tunnels. When everyone was asleep he set the tub at the foot of his bed for safekeeping. Around two o'clock in the morning, we heard the screams and found him flailing on top of his bed, eyes wild with panic.

"Mamá, they're eating me! Mamáááááá!"

Mamá and I rushed to him and found him covered with fire ants. She picked him up, took him outside and started brushing the ants off. They were everywhere, even in his hair. She poured a bucket of water over his head, washing away most of the reddish-black little monsters. After we dried him off and picked off the last few ants, I cut a piece of aloe, peeled back its rough exterior and rubbed the cool salve on his bites. Mamá wrapped him in a blanket, held him on her lap and sang to him softly until he fell asleep again.

I walk faster and pull the *empanada* out of my front apron pocket, take a bite and round the bend.

Tomás is on all fours, the upper half of his body behind a large rock.

"Tomás, what are you doing?"

"Sshhh . . . I found some big bugs. Come see! I woke them up, and now they're fighting!"

I step around the rock. He's poking a stick at two gold-colored scorpions. The black tips of their pincers and tails curve up over their armored bodies as they circle each other in a deadly dance. The *empanada* slips from my hand.

"Don't do that!" I shriek, but the words sound far away.

He turns his head to look at me and his hands slide backward across the dirt as I lurch forward with out-stretched arms. His eyes fly open, his mouth twists and he screams.

"It bit me! Evangelina!"

What do I do? Don't panic, don't panic, don't panic.

"It will be all right Tomás," I assure him in a trembling voice. "Papá will know what to do. We should get home now, but we must walk quickly."

He looks at me with eyes wide as saucers.

"You can do it. I'll hold your other hand."

"I don't like that bug." He sniffles and breathes in short choppy spurts as he swallows his tears.

"You're being very brave. We will be home soon, but we need to go faster, okay?"

His short legs try to keep up, but he stops and pulls his hand out of mine. The sting looks red and puffy.

"What's wrong with my hand?" Solitary teardrops become a tiny moving river.

"You remember when you bumped your head the other day on Mamá's sewing box, and that spot got swollen? That's all it is, but it will be okay. We have to get going, though. Come on."

He starts to walk alongside me again, feet dragging, but soon stops. I gently pull him along. Drops of sweat appear and multiply on his face.

"My throat feels . . . funny . . . " he says. "I can't, I can't . . . " He drops my hand.

I scoop him up and run. His tiny body softens and his head falls backward.

"Tomás! Hang on, we're almost there," I sob.

"Papá, come quick! Tomás! A scorpion . . . his hand," I heave in and out.

Papá takes Tomás from my arms and bounds inside the house. He lays Tomás on the sofa. Tomás' breath is uneven—short breath, deep breath, shallow gasp. Tiny bubbles gather at the corners of his mouth.

"Get some water!" Papá shouts.

I run to the back of the house and grab the water pitcher. I hold it out for Papá as he removes a small, folded knife from his front pocket and lays it by Tomás' legs. He pours water over the wound in a steady stream. The water dribbles off and forms a puddle on the floor.

"Find the mezcal and hurry!"

The bottle of mezcal hides in the cupboard behind bags of dried corn. Papá pours the mezcal over the blade, then cuts an X into the top of Tomás' hand. He pours the mezcal over it, lowers his head and puts his mouth over the wound. Papá sucks in the blood and venom and spits it out into his handkerchief. He props up Tomás' arm with a small pillow, elbow next to his body, hand in the air.

"Tomás, can you hear me? *M'ijito?* I am going to take care of you, and Mamá should be home soon."

The back screen door opens and Enrique walks in. Papá shouts, "Go get Doctor Gonzales!" Enrique glances at Tomás and bolts through the door. The clatter of hooves starts loud and fades.

Mamá swings the front door open with Domingo trailing behind her.

"Domingo, you're a big boy. Can you take this for me?" She smiles as she leans down to transfer a melon to his extended arms. Her eyes shift and lock onto Papá's, then rests on Tomás.

She drops the melon. "Evangelina, take Domingo outside!" she commands. "No, wait! Bring my rosary."

It hangs on her bedpost, where it always is. The long patterned sequence of large and small wooden beads and tiny silver medals adjoin a silver crucifix at the bottom. Every night Mamá kneels, fingers each bead on the rosary and repeats the Hail Mary and Lord's Prayer in their proper order to thank the Mother of God for her blessings and invite her to pray for our safety and salvation. Today, she will pray for her son's life.

I grab it and run back to Mamá. She brushes the back of her hand lightly across Tomás' forehead. I thrust the rosary at her.

"I let him go ahead without me. . . . I wasn't watching him. Please forgive me! It's my fault. I'm so sorry!"

"Take Domingo outside." She clasps the rosary and prays, "Our Father who art in heaven, hallowed be Thy name . . . "

"Does Tomás have a tummy ache?" Domingo whimpers.

"He'll be fine," I answer. Salty tears burn as they trickle down my raw, aching throat.

We walk into the dust-filled wind. Perfect yellow-pink grapefruit weigh down the branches of a tree loaded with God's bounty. I yank one off and tear into the thick fleshy rind. A million particles of citrus mist make the air smell sweet, but the taste in my mouth is bitter. Domingo pulls the grapefruit apart and bites into one half. Juice drips from his face and hands.

We sit against the tree trunk, him on one side, me on the other. My head drops to my chest. Tears fall onto my apron. They spread into the soft cotton fabric, each one a tiny circle of shame and regret.

Chapter Five
La Llorona

May 24, 1911

The knobs in the old woman's spine protrude beneath her gray cloak like miniature fists trying to break free. Her back stoops. Pale, wrinkled skin hangs from her exposed lanky arms. Her palms extend toward the threatening sky—long, frail fingers curve upward—stiff, pleading for something, waiting for something.

She hobbles away from me slowly. A hood shrouds her face. She emits a wail so sorrowful, so penetrating and hopeless, every muscle in my body tenses and a sudden chill washes over me. My heartbeat slows, thump . . . thump . . . thump . . . thump . . . thump.

I follow her with light steps, afraid she'll turn around. She moans, "Where are my babies? What have you done with my babies?"

The steep, narrow path leads us away from the cliff top down to the Rio Bravo. She does not look down as she walks, although the ground is uneven. The roots of the pinion trees stretch across as if carefully placed to make unsuspecting daydreamers fall to their watery deaths below. No need to watch her step. The old woman has walked this path thousands of times before.

She stops, turns her head and listens. My legs don't move except to shake from the inside out. I inhale and exhale a tiny stream of air, soundlessly. The river rushes below.

Her wild, menacing eyes settle on me, but nothing registers. My heart thunders in my chest. Surely she must hear it! If she doesn't see or hear me, maybe I am not flesh and blood but a soul adrift.

I follow the woman down, down, down to the river. The water surges and swirls. She hunches over the water's edge and reaches for something with expectant arms. Her gnarled fingers skim the water.

The woman . . . Who is she? My memory stirs and murky thoughts clear and crystallize.

La Llorona! Every child has heard the legend of the beautiful but vain woman abandoned by her husband. In a moment of desperation, blind with hatred toward the man who broke her heart, she stood at the edge of a cliff and silenced her children forever. Tortured by what she'd done, she jumped to her own death, hoping to reunite with her beloved son and daughter. But, even in the afterlife, she could not find them. So, every night she walks the riverbanks, in search of her babies, shrieking and sending dread through the souls of all who hear her. That is why they call her, "La Llorona," "the weeping woman" who mourns her loss and carries eternal shame for destroying those who were innocent and needed her the most.

From the swirling, life-giving waters, she plucks a small boy. My shame becomes so thick and heavy, the ground shifts, and I begin to sink. A strangled scream escapes my mouth, "Tomás!"

The old woman whips around, her crazed silver and white eyes fixed on mine. The face I see is my own. I scream again, but there is no sound, only the rush of the wind.

I bolt straight up. My nightgown sticks to me, limp with sweat. "Tomás!" I scream.

Mamá opens the door and peers in.

"Evangelina?" Her hair hangs loose and fans all around her shoulders. "M'ija, you've been crying? Hush now, my love, it was just a bad dream. I know this has been very hard for you, but what happened to your brother was not your fault. You must remember that. It was not your fault."

She walks to the bed, sits down and rests her cool hand on my shoulder. "Your father has him on the front porch in the rocking chair. Doctor Gonzales says he should regain his strength in a few days."

"May I go see him?"

"He's been asking for you."

I bounce out of bed and run outside. Tomás sits on Papá's lap, his back against Papá's chest, arms loose at his sides. Abuelito sits next to him and strokes Tomás' good hand.

"Tomás, are you feeling better?"

My eyes drop to the strips of cloth tied around his wounded hand. Blood fans out like a miniature red wildflower.

He strains to lift his head. He's pale as a dove. "Lina, did you keep the bug? I want to see it."

"No, Tomás, I did not keep the bug, and I hope I never see it again!" I run my hand over his tangled curls.

"He's already looking better, don't you think?" Elsa asks hopefully.

"The pink is back in his cheeks," Emilio lies.

"Tomás, you had an argument with some ants not long ago, and you lost! You're so sweet, the bugs can't resist you," Enrique cackles at his own bad joke.

Mamá casts him a glance with those angry eyes she uses with such great effect. Enrique clamps his mouth closed. I wish it would stay that way.

Tomás attempts a smile and drifts off to sleep. Emilio carries him back to his bed. I trail behind, kneel at his bedside and pray. Occasional jerky movements of his legs interrupt his rest. Maybe his dreams haunt him, too.

La Llorona flickers in and out of my thoughts like an open flame taunted by a wisp of wind. Thin gray lips sag at the corners. Sunken eyes gape at me from under a dark cloak. I shake the thought of La Llorona out of my head. It's just a ridiculous tale used to scare children into staying by their parents' sides and nothing else.

But, just in case, I stand guard over my brother until the dark completely consumes the light.

Chapter Six
Tamales

May 25, 1911

Tomás sleeps in our parents' room, like he does most days and nights. The rest of us sit at the table eating stew with chicken, garlic, squash, tomatoes and corn. The clatter of forks on plates sounds tinny and dull. Elsa stares vacantly out the window.

"You haven't eaten much, Elsa," Mamá comments. "Aren't you feeling well?"

"I've been thinking," she answers glumly. "Estela Morelos' family's moving to California."

"Why is that?" Mamá asks.

"Customers at her father's cantina say the war is moving north. Maybe we should cancel the *quinceañera* and leave town, like them," Elsa says.

Now, everyone knows.

Enrique crosses his arms and leans back. "That's crazy. We're not going to leave the ranch! And even if we did, where would we go?"

Abuelito holds up his hand. "Take it easy everyone. I've been talking with ranchers passing through the area. The revolution *is* growing, which has our president so worried he may even leave the country. That could improve the situation dramatically, but are your Papá and I concerned? Yes. Will we cancel the fiesta? No. The *quinceañera* has been planned for months."

"If Estela's family is leaving, do you think others will go, too?" I ask.

"I don't care what other people do," Enrique barks. "I'm not scared of the soldiers, and I will not be forced out!"

Abuelito grabs my hand under the table and gives it a gentle squeeze. "Hundreds, maybe even thousands will leave Mexico. Others don't feel there's any real danger. They want to protect what little they have. Others are too sick or too old to leave, like me. We will not base our decisions on what others choose. Now, enough serious talk. After lunch I'm going for a walk. I've got *dulce de camote* in my pocket. Who wants to join me?"

"I'll go!" Enrique and Domingo call out in unison. Sweet potato candy works every time with the boys.

May 26, 1911

Mamá hovers over the wood stove. Strings of dried chilies and garlic and a carved wooden *Cristo* decorate the stove hood. Iron wall racks hold spoons and various-sized ladles and whisks. Jars of peppercorns, cloves, cinnamon sticks and carved gourd bowls and clay cups line the scallop-edged shelves.

She peers into a vast iron cauldron and shreds a large chunk of pork with two giant serving forks, then spoons in a dark paste made of freshly toasted cumin seeds, garlic, oregano, dried red chili and water, crushed and mixed in the *molcajete*. Making tamales involves the whole family: the young, the old, even the ones who don't like to cook or who don't want to cook. Some of Mamá's church friends will join us this afternoon to help.

Mamá mixes the cornmeal dough with hot pork broth, salt, lard and melted pork fat in a separate pot. There's so much of it, and it's so thick that she uses both hands to stir with an enormous wooden spoon then gives up. She pushes a loose hair off her forehead with the back of her arm, walks to the front door and calls, "Adán, I need you in here."

Papá stomps his boots outside to loosen the dirt and sets his hat on the rocking chair just outside the screen door before he comes in. He leans over Mamá's shoulder and pecks her cheek.

"Do you need me to taste anything? You know, check the spices?" He smacks his lips.

Mamá grabs a clean spoon, dips it in, brings up a mouthful and feeds it to Papá. She raises her eyebrows and awaits the review.

"*Muy sabroso*, Maríaelena. You have outdone yourself again. Is that all you needed? A taster? I make an excellent taster," he says, raising the spoon to dip it back into the pot.

"No, no, no," Mamá scolds him, taking the spoon from his hand. "If all I needed was a taster, I could have done that myself. I need you to *mix* the *masa*. I can't stir it anymore. Wash up."

I take my seat, grab a stack of corn husks and set them down on my left. When Mamá decides the *masa* has the right, light and fluffy texture, she fills a bowl and sets it on my right.

"Okay *m'ija*, don't spread it too thick."

I hold an *hoja* in one hand, the widest end pointing toward me. I spread the *masa* downward from the middle of the husk to the widest end and leave the upper, narrower part of the *hoja* plain, with no *masa* at all. Mamá adds a thin line of meat to the center of each tamal, rolls it tightly from the long side, folds the top of the *hoja* down to make a perfect tube-shaped bundle, grabs a small finger full of *masa* and seals the open end. Mamá takes a thin strip of hoja and ties it around bundles of six tamales and stacks the bundles in a pile.

Papá lines an oversized pot with *hojas* with an upside down *molcajete* and water at the bottom. He carefully situates tamales around the *molcajete* in an upside down V and takes them outside to steam over a fire.

Elsa finds a place at the table. "Good morning," she says.

"Elsa, I've finalized the menu for Wednesday," Mamá announces. "Now, I have to figure out how to make enough food for fifty people!"

Elsa's eyes open wide. "Will there really be fifty people?"

"Well, there are the neighbors, plus René and his family, if his mother can make it. Father Roberto and everyone from church. And oh, yes, the Treviño family said they'll come."

Tiny bursts of gold flicker in Elsa's eyes.

"A girl from church has been helping around their house ever since Señor Treviño and the oldest brother were kidnapped by the *villistas*," I add. "I'm surprised the rest of them are coming, because my friend says the señora stays in bed all day and talks to no one."

Rodrigo, the second oldest son, and one of the most handsome boys in town, has had his eye on Elsa for years. She stares at him at church when he's not looking and blushes when he catches her doing it.

"Well, that *is* surprising." Elsa studies the kitchen floor. "Will Rodrigo come, too?"

"*La pobre* señora, it'll be good for her to get out of the house and put her worries aside, even if just for a day. And yes, Rodrigo's the man of the house now and must accompany his mother and siblings. Besides, you've known each other for many years. You must be pleased, *m'ijita*."

"Mamá, Rodrigo and I are acquaintances from church, that's all," she responds.

When she finally looks up, I wink at her and watch her turn red as a radish.

Chapter Seven
Quinceañera

May 28, 1911

Despite all the worries and extra work, the excitement in the house today is thick as refried beans.

I pull on my fullest petticoat, long gray skirt, a white blouse with extra puffy sleeves, ruffled socks and Mamá's old black school shoes with an open V shape on the top. Three buttons form a row on each side of the V. Stretchy bands loop around each button and attach to the button on the opposite side.

The carved wooden chest at the foot of my bed holds quilts, some old dolls, doll clothes and a cigar box full of ribbons. I part my hair down the middle, weave two dark blue ribbons into two braids and pin them across the top of my head. A small spray of tiny white blossoms from the orange tree goes behind my ear, even though they're already starting to wilt.

Sun streams through the sheer white curtains of the sewing room window, and the room glows with soft light. Elsa turns to the left, then to the right as she admires her dress in the full length mirror. What a stir it will cause! Made of white cotton with hand-made lace and delicate, sky-blue embroidered butterflies, the skirt cascades in three layers, the second and third layers longer than the one before it. Bluebell flowers adorn the hemline of each tier. Mamá spent night after candle-lit night in her rocking chair making the unique lace pattern of the bodice and sleeves with each pull of the thread. Each stitch forms part of the subtle lace landscape—miniature flowers, vines and leaves surrounded by tightly spaced crisscrosses, each one smaller than a grain of rice.

Francisca sits on Mamá's sewing chair and nods approvingly.

"Elsa, you look gorgeous, except for all those pin curls stuck to your head," I taunt.

"Must you always say what crosses your mind?" Francisca reprimands me then turns toward Elsa. "You want me to style your hair?"

"I was thinking of loose curls pinned on the top to make a bun, but leave some hanging down on the sides," Elsa suggests. "Something regal, like a princess."

Francisca lets Elsa's black, glossy curls fall loose. She takes sections of hair and folds them under to make a fancy bun, skillfully twisting the loose hair into two large curls with her fingers, one on each side, that fall over Elsa's shoulders and down the bodice of her dress.

Francisca hands me two abalone hair combs carved with ridges to look like clam shells. "You do this part, Evangelina. Put them in wherever you think they'll look best."

I push a comb in on each side of Elsa's perfect bun. Francisca opens the lipstick tube Mamá ordered all the way from Mexico City and adds a dab of pink to Elsa's full lips.

I clasp my hands and grin. "Can you believe it? The mass is less than two hours away, and you look perfect, Elsa."

"Thank you Evangelina, but I feel bad celebrating when Tomás is so sick," she sighs.

My stomach drops. How can I celebrate when Tomás isn't getting better?

"One of Mamá's friends will stay with him the whole time," Francisca says as she dabs her face with powder in a pretty silver case. "After the service, we'll come back and check on him, all night long if we want to. Not *you*, though, Elsa. Us. Your job is to be beautiful and charming and behave like an eligible maiden, ready for a young man to whisk you off to some happily ever after fairy tale life."

Friends and family fill the pews at Iglesia de la Paz. Elsa stands at the altar and scans the faces in the congregation.

Father Roberto walks in from a side door, greets Elsa and turns to us, Holy Bible in hand.

"Welcome all!" he begins in Latin. "Today we have gathered together to celebrate one of the most beautiful events of Mexican culture, the *quinceañera* Mass. Adán and Maríaelena de León welcome you to this joyous occasion. True to the promises they made when Adán and Maríaelena baptized her fifteen years ago in this very church, they have been Elsa's first teachers in the Christian faith and way of life. They have seen her develop her faith, and now they bring her here to give witness to their own faith in God. They pray to the Most High so that, through the wish of the Most Holy Virgin, Elsa will continue to follow the Lord's call with deep devotion.

"Elsa, in the name of the Catholic Church, I congratulate you on this important occasion. Will you honor God with the strength of conviction you inherited from your parents, your grandparents and all of your ancestors, and will you keep these promises to your family, friends, the Holy Virgin and the Lord our Savior?"

Elsa nods. "I will."

Father Roberto lifts his palms upward as a signal for the people to rise from their seats and join together in the Lord's Prayer.

After Mass, the ceremony is over. Elsa stands just beyond the church steps, and people surround her to offer congratulations, give her hugs, pinch her cheeks and tell her how beautiful she is. My parents stand close by and beam with pride.

Our mules Félix and Felipe pull the wagon home on the same path they've followed to and from the church for ten years. We hop off and scurry around with last-minute preparations as guests stream in. Papá, Abuelito and the boys built a dance floor surrounded by four wooden posts three meters high. They covered it with a thick white canvas roof that drapes down a half meter on each side. Flowers made of brightly colored tissue paper—sky blue, brilliant pink and sunny yellow—adorn the edges of the fabric overhang. On the inside of the structure the flowers hang from strings of varying lengths and float in the breeze. Twenty lanterns with soft glowing light surround the yard. Fireflies move through the air like floating sparkles. Soon it'll be dark enough to see them weave and dance in the warm, sticky air. Tables are arranged around the yard with sweet smelling magnolia blooms in small copper vases. A long table by the back porch holds the food and drinks. A smaller table holds two oblong clay dishes of bread pudding. Mamá mixed the bread, eggs, walnuts, cinnamon, raisins, milk and sugar last night and baked each pan for an hour in the outdoor clay oven. Three more pans sit in the house.

Elsa spots me from across the yard, waves and bounces over. "I've been greeting the guests as they arrive. There are so many! I just checked on Tomás. Señora Salinas from church is telling him stories. He seems about the same."

"Yes, I checked on . . . "

Elsa grabs my arm and covers her mouth. "Look over there," she motions with her head, "but *don't* turn around too suddenly."

"I can barely understand you with your hand over your mouth," I whine.

I swivel nonchalantly, look across the crowd, and see Rodrigo and his mother approaching. Elsa's face becomes whiter. Mamá skips down the back porch steps and catches up to them.

"Elsa, isn't it nice Señora Treviño and Rodrigo could make it tonight?" Mamá says.

I prod Elsa with my elbow.

"Yes, of course," she stammers. "It's so nice of you to come. Where are the little ones?"

"A family friend came for a few days," Señora Trevino answers. "She's watching after the children. As you know, I have not been well since my husband and son were taken by the *villistas,* but I felt we really must offer our congratulations."

"Gracias, señora," Elsa replies.

Mamá picks up the señora's hand and cups it tenderly. "I hope you don't think I'm intruding, but I must ask. Have you heard any word from your husband and Martín? We've been quite concerned."

"There's been no word. We think they went south, but can't say where. I am sick with worry, but luckily," she looks squarely at Elsa, "Rodrigo is a strong, responsible son, and he is taking care of the family until their safe return."

Mamá nods. "We will pray for them as we have every night. Please let us know if we can be of any help. But of course, tonight, we celebrate Elsa. She looks beautiful, no?"

"Ahem," Rodrigo clears his throat. "I agree, you look especially beautiful tonight. Your gown makes you look elegant . . . I mean you always look elegant."

"You are very kind," Elsa replies. "You know, the maria-chis will be here soon, and then the dancing will begin."

"Will you honor me with the first dance? I mean, after you dance with your father?" He swings his golden brown hair away from his forehead revealing large hazel eyes and long lashes.

Elsa looks at Mamá.

"That is for your father to decide, Elsa," Mamá says.

"Rodrigo, I would be happy to dance with you, but I must ask Papá first."

"Perhaps it would be more customary if I asked your father myself," Rodrigo offers. "Will you wait for me?"

"Yes, of course." Elsa blushes.

Oh, how romantic! He's so handsome. Those eyes! Those eyelashes! When will my turn come to find a boy? Someone tall and strong, with striking eyes, broad shoulders, long fingers and a brilliant smile. And, funny, hard-working and a true gentleman like my father. A girl can always dream.

Mamá and Rodrigo's mother talk quietly. Elsa and I watch Rodrigo approach our father. They speak briefly and shake hands.

The guests ravage the food within the first hour. Francisca and I re-fill the platters with tamales and *biscochitos*. Mamá scrambles to make another giant batch of rice. I pick up empty plates and work my way to the kitchen. I set them in the sink as the music starts. I run through the back door and over to the edge of the yard. The music grows louder as the mariachis stroll in one after the other in a single file line with their instruments: a *guitarrón*, two trumpets, two guitars, two violins and an accordion. The performers join in harmony to sing one of my favorite songs, "Adiós, Mamá Carlota." Next, the band strikes up "Alejandra," a Mexican waltz, and people gather round the dance floor. Papá extends his hand to Elsa, and they begin the traditional father-daughter dance. The song ends, Papá bows, and Elsa curtsies. He pulls up a chair, stands on it and speaks in a loud, clear voice.

"May I have your attention, please? I would like to toast my daughter, Elsa. *M'ija*, your mother and I are very proud of the young woman you have become. You deserve all the happiness the good Lord can bestow upon you. Congratulations, *m'ija*! A toast, to Elsa!"

The crowd lifts their glasses. "To Elsa!"

"More music!" my father shouts.

The band starts again with another waltz, "Sobre las Olas." Rodrigo steps forward, nods to Papá and takes Elsa's hand.

"May I have this dance?" he asks and bows.

"You may." Elsa curtsies.

My heart flips.

They take their places in the middle of the dance floor. She places her left hand behind his back, and his right arm curves around hers. Her right hand extends out to hold his left hand, although their hands barely touch. They glide and twirl, never taking their eyes off each other. Several ladies cluck about what a lovely couple they make. I can barely breathe.

The song ends and Rodrigo leads Elsa away from the dance floor to an old fig tree that's nearby. He leans in, says something, and she puts her face next to his ear and says something back. They join hands!

I eat a helping of tamales to pass the time. Then a second helping. Finally, Elsa ambles back to the fiesta.

"What did you talk about? Did he tell you he loves you?" I ask.

"He said he . . . cares about me. I mean, he has feelings for me." She looks down and fingers the layers of her gown.

"Come on! What *kind* of feelings does he have for you?"

"Keep it down. Now, promise you won't tell anyone."

"I promise!" Elsa's found love!

"Later tonight he's going to ask Papá for permission to court me."

A commotion erupts along the side of the house. Horses whinny.

"Who are you? What do you want here?" a man hollers.

"Soldiers!" a boy yells.

Two thin, bearded men in dirty soldiers' coats make their way into the crowd. Sombreros shroud their faces.

"Por favor, don't be afraid," the taller man announces. "I am Pedro Treviño and this is Martín, my son." Both men remove their hats.

A thunder of happy voices fills the air.

"Thank God!"

"Welcome, Pedro!"

"How did you escape?"

Señora Treviño and Rodrigo push their way through. She drops to her knees, bends over and holds her hands to her face.

"I didn't know if you were alive," she sobs.

Señor Treviño crouches down and helps her to her feet. He puts his hand to his wife's cheek and wraps an arm around her. Martín grins and smacks Rodrigo on the shoulder.

"I'm sure most of you know my oldest boy and I were kidnapped last month, but we escaped," Señor Treviño begins. "We stopped at the church on the way into town to warn Father Roberto that Villa's men may be looking for us. He said we'd find many of you here."

The crowd erupts in nervous conversation.

"Listen to me!" he commands. "It was only a matter of time. Mariposa cannot escape the revolution. It is coming. I'm sorry to be the bearer of such bad news. I am especially sorry if our return makes the situation worse. It's up to you whether you stay or go, but regardless of your decision, you must take whatever means is necessary to protect yourselves. Do not delay."

Mothers call for their children. Fathers scatter to prepare their horses. Some hastily call out their goodbyes as they scurry away. Others leave without a word.

Rodrigo runs over and grabs Elsa's hand again. "I will see you soon. And I *will* speak with your father, but I have to go now. I'm sorry. Thank you for the dance. Don't forget what I said. I meant every word."

He makes his way back to his parents and brother, looks over his shoulder and waves.

Elsa watches him until he's out of sight, then joins Enrique, Emilio and me standing in a huddle.

"What will happen now?" Elsa whispers.

"Let everyone clear out," Emilio answers. "Then we'll talk with Papá. He'll know what to do. But I don't think he's going to tell us to sit around and wait for the soldiers to arrive."

Chapter Eight
The Box

May 28, 1911

A little girl's corn husk doll lies on the ground by the table stacked with unused plates and silverware. A cream-colored shawl drapes over the back of a chair. A sombrero and a lone shoe lay next to the dance floor.

"Papá said to clean up later. He wants us inside now," Enrique orders as he lumbers past me with a stack of dishes in his arms.

Everyone files into the living room and finds a place on the sofa or the floor. Papá holds a sleeping Tomás over his shoulder. Abuelito leans on his cane next to him. Mamá sits in a chair nervously twisting a handkerchief. Papá walks a few paces, leans down and smoothly shifts Tomás to Mamá.

"*Hijos míos*, I'm afraid Señor Treviño confirmed what I hoped would never happen. The whole country is at war." Papá gently touches Mamá's shoulder. "We don't live on an hacienda with expensive things, and we work the land ourselves, but we may be targets *because* we own land. We must leave Mexico. There is no other way."

Leave and go where?

"What does the revolution have to do with us?" Enrique asks. "We're a simple farming town!"

"They want supplies—food, ammunition, horses and cattle. They take whatever they need or want. They also want young men to serve as soldiers. Pedro and Martín were very lucky to escape. Most are not so lucky."

"Is leaving the country the only choice we have?" Emilio asks.

"It's the safest choice," Papá responds. He runs his fingers through his dark curly hair. "We'll go up north into the United States. Your tía Cristina and her husband Mario live in Texas. They have a little girl, Leticia. Your mother sent your aunt a letter a week ago saying we might be coming, although we didn't think it would be this soon. We'll only stay there until I can find work and a place of our own. When the war is over, we'll come back to the ranch and start again."

"Your father and I will start packing tonight," says Mamá. "We'll leave Tuesday before sunrise."

"I'll help Papá with the mules and prepare the wagon," Emilio offers.

"I'll help you prepare food, pack up the kitchen and whatever else you need," says Francisca.

"What's happening, Mamá?" Tomás asks sleepily.

"Nothing, go back to sleep, *m'ijo,*" Mamá says as she shoots Papá a worried glance.

⌁⌁⌁

I sit on my bed and draw my knees close to my chest. I grab my favorite doll, Belinda, close my eyes and rock back and forth. Elsa peeks in, her cheeks stained with tears.

"This can't be happening." I shake my head. Elsa sits next to me on the bed, grabs my hand, and we sit quietly for a moment. "I don't want to go."

"Me either," she murmurs. "Rodrigo and I . . . "

I stretch out across my bed and use my pillow to stifle the sound of my crying.

"I'm going to clean up outside. I'll drag Enrique out there with me. I'll tell Mamá you're not feeling well," Elsa whispers and closes the door.

I should be helping pack or cleaning up the mess, but I give up and give in to my tired eyes, tired body, tired mind and let myself drift into the blackness.

La Llorona points at me. "Look after your brother," she cackles. She comes toward me and whooshes through my body like the wind.

⟶

May 29, 1911

I stagger out of bed. Flutters fill my stomach like a swarm of moths beating my insides in search of light. My family gets up and moves around with very little talking among us. My parents let Tomás and Domingo sleep.

"I'm sorry about how the *quinceañera* ended," I say to Elsa in the hallway between the kitchen and our bedroom. "It was perfect, until the end."

"It was special, wasn't it? And Rodrigo, well, I'm only sorry it lasted just one night."

"He'll be here waiting for you when we come back."

"I hope so. There's still a lot to do. We better keep moving." She turns and wipes a tear away with the back of her hand.

While the rest of us slept, Mamá and Francisca packed sacks of corn and beans, strips of salted dried meat, quilts, herbs, roots and teas for healing, family portraits, soap, pots, pans, knives, chairs, chests and two small tables. One wooden crate or suitcase per person for everything else. That means two changes of clothes, a coat, shoes and a few other small items for the boys and two or three more things like a favorite hat or extra pair of shoes for the girls.

I set a small brown suitcase on my bed. Papá and Abuelito talk outside my open window.

"I heard Villa's men are closing in. The sooner we leave, the better. I will miss you, but it'll be especially hard for the children. We'll pray for your safety every night and day."

I race outside and throw my arms around Abuelito. "You'll be killed if you stay here!"

Papá and Abuelito look at each other, startled.

"*M'ija*, I didn't know you were listening," says Papá. "Abuelito will stay with Francisca and René at an old house less than a day's travel from here. It was René's uncle's place, and it's well hidden on an abandoned property. He won't let anything happen to Francisca or your grandfather."

"Francisca's not coming either? Don't say that! The soldiers are coming! You said it yourself!"

"René's mother is too ill to travel. Her heart is weak. Francisca must take care of her and René's little brothers and sisters. The old house is on a hill where René's uncle grew coffee beans many years ago. It's been empty since René was a boy. It's the perfect place to go unnoticed."

I kneel on the ground, wrap my arms around my sides and weep. My perfect, predictable life is slipping away.

Abuelito nods at Papá. "Let me talk to her," he says. "Lina, let me help you up."

He pulls me to my feet. I follow alongside him as he takes one hobbled step after another.

"Evangelina, each night I pray to God and thank Him for His blessings. I ask Him to keep my family safe, and so far, He has answered my prayers. I have no reason to doubt Him now. He has a plan for all of us, and I accept whatever God's plan is for me."

"God's plan is for you to come with us!"

He puts his hands on my shoulders. "Mariposa is the only home I've ever known. Your abuelita is buried on this ranch, and I will not leave her. I visit her grave and talk to her every day. Sometimes I take her a piece of fruit or a bunch of wildflowers, but I often tell her how proud I am of you, your brothers and sisters, and what fine people you all are. I find great comfort in that."

I hug him tightly, and my warm tears soak into his soft cotton shirt. He pats my back gently like Mamá does when she's trying to get Domingo to go to sleep.

"Your father is waiting for me, and René will be here soon. Your father insists on giving us instructions for the cattle, even though we know what to do. But, if it makes your papá feel better, then we'll let him explain it to us. I'll just have to pretend I'm listening." He winks. "I must go or I'll be late. Be brave, m'ija. You have great inner strength. You just have to reach deeper to find it."

"I don't want to leave you," I cry. "Please come with us."

He shakes his head. "I'm sorry, *m'ija*, but I can't. Now, listen to me . . . " His voice drops to a whisper. "Before you leave tomorrow, I have something important to ask of you, and our conversation must be private. Let's find a quiet place after dinner, eh?"

⸺⸺⸺

The day's activity winds down. Domingo trails behind as Mamá moves around the house and takes care of last-minute details.

"Pick me up," he implores. "I'm sleepy."

"I'll take him, Mamá," I say. "We'll go for a walk."

"Oh, thank you, Evangelina."

Sections of hair hang free from Mamá's normally perfect braid, and the front of her apron shows signs of the past two day's meals.

She musters a half smile. "Don't stay out long. It's past his bedtime, and I'd like you to get to bed soon, too. Tomorrow will be a long day for all of us."

I hoist Domingo up, open the screen door and step out into the thick, sweet smelling air. The grapefruit trees would have been harvested next week. Mamá told Francisca to let the church congregation know they can take whatever they want. It would be a shame for it to go to waste.

I pat Félix and Felipe outside the stable and step inside. Álvaro, my favorite horse, stands in his stall. His dark coat shines even in the dim light. I use my free hand to rub the soft spot of his muzzle. Domingo reaches out, and I angle my body slightly so he can touch him, too.

"Be careful. Touch him here." I direct his hand to Álvaro's thick muscled neck. "If you put your hand too close to his mouth, he may think it's something to eat!"

I lean in and whisper, "I'm sorry, Álvaro. You can't go with us. Papá says you're too old to make the trip, but I don't believe that for one moment." I scratch behind his ears. "René and Francisca will take good care of you. I'd take you if I could." The tears start again.

Domingo's head droops, and his warm breath spreads over my shoulder. I carefully lower myself onto a bale of hay in the corner of the stable to rest my arms and back. If I had something comfortable to lean on, I could surely fall asleep, but after a few minutes, I summon my last bit of energy, stand up and reposition Domingo in my arms. Abuelito enters the stable with the light of the moon behind him.

"Abuelito, you startled me!"

"Evangelina, now is our only chance to talk in private, so listen very carefully." His voice is so low I can barely hear it. "I have something to give you. You must take it to Texas, but you cannot tell anyone, not even your parents."

"Forgive me, Abuelito, I don't understand."

He looks around the barn and peers outside the doorway. "Many years ago I did something." He pauses. "I found something when I was a young man. I've had it hidden for a long time. I'll never be able to use it here. I'm too old now. Your family will need it. You must hide it where no one can find it. Do you understand?"

I nod my head, but I don't understand at all.

He walks to the back of Álvaro's stall, kneels, sweeps the hay away with his hand and yanks on a loose floorboard. He lifts out a reddish-brown colored wooden box that looks eerily like a miniature casket tied in both directions with thick string. It's no more than ten centimeters deep, about as long as my forearm and as wide as my hand from my little finger to my thumb with my fingers spread out.

Abuelito pushes himself up. The usual twinkle in his eye is gone, replaced with a grim face I hardly recognize. "Do not open this, Evangelina." He nods toward the box. "Once your family gets settled, I will instruct your father what to do."

"What's in it?"

"It's better for you not to know. If the wrong people find out about it, it can mean danger for you all. We have a special bond, you and me, and that is why I've asked you to do this important task."

With his one free arm he kisses his fingers and softly presses them to my cheek. "I'll take your brother in the house."

He sets the box on the bale of hay I was just sitting on, lifts Domingo off my shoulder and gently sets him down. "Come on, m'ijo, it's time to get in bed. I'll walk with you."

"Hmmm? Where is Lina?" Domingo asks.

"I'll come inside soon," I assure him.

My heart beats furiously inside my chest, and my mouth goes dry as the desert ground. What is in the box, and why is Abuelito asking me to take it if it's so dangerous? I'm frightened, but I look around and lift the box carefully. It's not too heavy. Everything inside me wants to open it, but I resist. A striped blue and gray wool blanket hangs over Álvaro's stall and the next stall over. I grab it, fold it and set the box in between the layers.

Chapter Nine
Until Next Time

May 30, 1911

I lie on my side curled up tight.

"Evangelina, you've got to get ready," a voice says.

I open my eyes and close them again. "Not yet . . . " I mumble.

"Lina, wake up." Francisca sits on the edge of my bed and gently shakes my shoulder.

"What time is it?"

"It's three o'clock. Papá wants to get on the road early. You should be able to board the train in Los Pinos tonight, but Papá and Emilio have a long way to go after that."

"How long?"

I don't like the thought of splitting off from my father and brother, not one bit, but the train won't be an option for them. They'll have the mules, the wagon and all our things.

"At least a week, if not longer. It depends on the conditions of the roads, and if there's any . . . " She looks at me and through me at the same time. "Ummm . . . I've prepared a basket of bread and *empanadas*, and René squeezed grapefruit for an hour last night, so there's enough to last a few days. We put it all in the chest on the back of the wagon."

I sit up and lean my head against her chest.

"Evangelina, you must go, you know that. René and I would join you if his mother was not so ill. Besides, I have to take care of Abuelito. I'll make sure he eats well, and if it's safe, we'll take him to church. He'll come back to the ranch every now and then and help René with the cattle. He'll stay busy. Things will turn out all right. You'll get along well in Texas. Before long, you'll fit right in with the other girls your age. They'll love you. Think of it as an adventure. Texas, the United States! Tall buildings, fancy cars, fancy clothes. You'll have to send me a letter and tell me all about it." She reaches out and touches my arm. "You best get going."

We walk down the hall hand in hand. Papá stands by the bedroom door. Mamá steps out and closes the door behind her. Her chin falls to her chest and tears stream down her face.

"Adán," she sputters. "Doctor Gonzales says Tomás . . . he says . . . Tomás . . . he's lost too much weight, and he's still weak. Doctor Gonzales says he can't go with us. Please don't make me leave him! I can't . . . "

Francisca drops my hand and runs to Mamá. "I will take care of him! When the war is over, Papá can come back for him . . . or maybe René's mother will be better, and we'll go to Texas. We could bring him to you! Please, Mamá, don't cry."

Mamá looks up. "Heavenly Father, why are you punishing us?" she demands. "Have we not been faithful servants?" She turns to Francisca. "M'ija, I can't leave him behind. He needs me." She closes her eyes and sways back and forth like a dried-out stalk of corn in a fierce wind.

Papá grabs Mamá by the waist to steady her. "María-elena, none of us wanted this to happen, but we must do as the doctor says."

"He needs his mother!" she shouts.

"Maríaelena, listen to me," Papá continues. "You and the children will try to board the train in Los Pinos tonight, but there are no guarantees you'll even get on. What would you do if Tomás got worse without a doctor nearby?" He grabs Mamá's shoulders and kisses her on the forehead. "René will take Tomás, Francisca, Abuelito and his family to that abandoned house until he is sure the soldiers will not be passing through here or until they've come and gone. They'll keep Tomás safe, where Francisca can care for him and Doctor Gonzales can visit. We'd be risking his life if we took him with us." He searches Mamá's face for some sign of acceptance.

"How are we going to tell him?" she asks.

"We'll just have to tell him plain, but he can't see us cry," Papá cautions.

They hold each other for another moment, and then disappear into the bedroom. Francisca and I stay in the hallway and stare at each other numbly.

The front door opens, and Enrique pokes his head in.

"Evangelina," he shouts in his squeaky half-boy, half-man voice. "If your suitcase is not on the wagon, good luck finding a spot for it. Or are you not tall enough to see onto the wagon bed?"

"I'll be right there!"

I ignore the short comment, turn and run into my bedroom, one last time to pray.

Dear God,

You are the one I turn to for help in moments of weakness and times of need. I ask you to be with Tomás now. Please drive out all sickness from his body. It is I who have sinned. Tomás is an innocent child who loves you with all his heart. If someone is to be punished, let it be me. May you be glorified through his life and mine. All this I pray in the name of the Father, the Son and the Holy Ghost. Amen.

I throw my gray wool poncho over my head and clutch my doll Belinda. I promised myself I wouldn't take her, because I'm too old for dolls now, but last night, hours after the house went quiet, I opened the seam in her cloth back, removed the stuffing and inserted Abuelito's box. I pushed as much stuffing around the box as I could, sewed the seam back together and changed her into her christening outfit, the long white flowing gown and matching bonnet with the light blue ribbon. The gown should hide the stiffness and slightly odd shape of her once soft, perfectly formed body. I lift the two dresses I packed, lay Belinda down, cover her with the dresses, a shawl, close the suitcase, wrap a belt around it and cinch it tight.

———

The family gathers outside. Red splotches cover Mamá's face and neck.

"Tomás is too sick to travel. Francisca will care for him here until he's well enough to join us," she explains. "Say your goodbyes and pray for his return to good health. Then we will be on our way."

Emilio, Enrique and Elsa head inside to see Tomás. Mamá and Papá hug Abuelito and say their goodbyes. I hug Abuelito tightly and rest my cheek on his chest.

I shift to stand on the tips of my toes, and he bends down so I can whisper in his ear, "I will miss your smile, your stories, your silly jokes and everything else about you. Please say we will see each other again soon."

"*M'ijita*, come with me. There's time for a walk with your abuelito. I'll bring her right back," he assures my father.

I follow him out into the brush, past the orchard. We walk slowly, hand in hand, down the well-worn path surrounded by patches of bluebonnets. Abuelita's grave lies just ahead under the largest tree on the ranch, a cypress. Papá said it's hundreds of years old. There's a simple, arched headstone with the inscription: "Adelfa García de León Beloved Wife, Mother and Grandmother." Abuelito kneels, plucks a bluebonnet growing nearby and holds its thin, fragile stem in his thick, callused fingers.

"Adelfa, my loving wife. Our granddaughter wants me to promise that we will see each other again. Now, you taught me to never make promises I may not be able to keep. As much as I want to, I cannot say if Evangelina and I will see each other again. But if the good Lord's will is for me to see her again, then it will be so, and I will be eternally grateful. I bring our granddaughter here, because I want you to pray with me, to pray that she will grow into the remarkable woman we always knew she would be. It's true she's short, I mean not even tall enough to swat a fly halfway up the kitchen wall, but full of heart. She worries too much, and sometimes lets her fears hold her back from all that is possible. But with your help and God's grace, she'll build a life she can be proud of and do good for others. My dear Adelfa, I pray that she and the rest of our family will be safe and find happiness. I will be here again tomorrow, if I can. Truthfully, with all that's going on, I may not make it every day, but you are in my heart, every moment of every day. As always, I find comfort in your presence." He leans over and touches the gravestone. "In God's name we pray."

"I won't let you down, Abuelito." I press my palm to Abuelita's gravestone. "And, I'll pray for your safety and good health."

"May God be with you, my child," he says.

I walk away and turn around to look at Abuelito one last time. He casts a shadow much taller than himself across the swaying grasses.

I sob the whole way back to the house, gather my composure and walk into my parents' room to say goodbye to Tomás.

"Evangelina?" Tomás says weakly. "I want to go with you. Don't leave me here!" he wails like a wounded dog.

"This is not a goodbye, Tomás. It's *hasta luego*. May God bless you and keep you safe."

PART II

Chapter Ten

Departure

May 30, 1911

Papá taps Felipe's left hindquarters with his walking stick. "Yah!" he shouts. Félix and Felipe strain to make the wagon move. Papá runs up front to encourage them. They take a few short steps and stop. Papá walks backward and shouts again. "*¡Ándale! ¡Vámonos!*" It's not a myth. Mules really are stubborn.

The wagon hinges creak and groan like ancient Señora Chapa when she hobbles her way down the aisle at Sunday communion. Mamá, Elsa and I sit up front on the wooden bench seat on the folded blue and white quilt Abuelita gave Mamá and Papá on their wedding day. Domingo sits under the thick canvas cover, his legs drawn tightly up around him. Pots, candles, kindling wood, blankets, pillows, clothing, a rocking chair, two small tables, bed mats, barrels, food, plates, eating utensils and a spare wheel fill the wagon. Two rifles and boxes of ammunition lay against the inside edge of the wagon bed.

The mules get into a rhythm, their noses to the ground. Things jangle and bang loudly against each other.

Papá stays up front. Enrique and Emilio lag behind with the goats. Emilio holds the third rifle.

The orange barn cat darts out onto the trail and trots behind us.

"What do you think you're doing?" Enrique hollers. "Look! That dumb cat thinks it's coming with us!"

I found her six months ago and named her Rosalía. She showed up at the rancho from time to time but never stayed for long. She was all skin and bones at first, but now her middle is so big it nearly brushes the ground. I thought it was the fresh cream, straight from the cow to her dish, but it's obvious now she's pregnant. Tomás planned to name all the kittens Poncho.

We pick up speed. Rosalía quickens her pace for a moment, then slows down, turns and trots back toward the ranch until she's out of sight.

She's going home. Our home. My home. My home!

"Don't go!" I scream in my head. That cat is the last bit of home I'll see in a long time.

Tomás loves her, though. At least he'll get to see the kittens when he gets better.

But, Francisca doesn't know about the cat. I should have said something to Francisca before I left! Now it's too late!

"Can we turn back? Please?" I plead. "I didn't tell Francisca about the kittens. Tomás wanted to see the kittens!"

Mamá rubs my shoulders. "No, m'ija, we need to keep going. It took an hour to say our goodbyes, and we've got to get to the train station before dark. I don't think I can bear to go back then leave again, as much as I want to."

Elsa leans over and looks behind us. "I can't see the ranch anymore," she whispers. "Rodrigo and I danced back there two nights ago. Now, it's gone, like it was only a dream."

She stares ahead in silence. Mamá rubs my back some more.

For hours upon hours the wagon jerks and bumps over every rock and dip in the road until my backside aches. The farther we go, the emptier I feel. Even the land looks emptier. No trees, just sparse cactus, dry weeds, rocks and dirt. Shades of brown and gray in every direction. I haven't seen any animals—not a squirrel or rabbit in sight. Too hot and dry, I suppose. There must be animals out here, hiding in the shade, waiting for the sun to set and the hot air to lift. I shudder at the thought of my father and brother sleeping in a tent. A piece of canvas won't protect them against a bobcat or black bear.

May 31, 1911

The sun shines through the tall grimy windows of the Los Pinos Train Station where we'll board the northbound train, cross the border at Paloma and arrive in Seneca, Texas. From the looks of it, it's not much more than an open stretch of land and a train station with swaths of trees on each side of it.

We arrived too late last night to get on a train. Mamá, Elsa, Domingo and I slept in tents on hard, bumpy ground outside the station with what must have been a hundred other people who did the same. Some looked like they'd been here for a while with simple lean-tos to cover them, clotheslines strung between trees, kerosene lamps, pots and pans strewn about and garbage everywhere.

Despite my aching, tired body, the sound of bats calling to each other as they circled overhead kept me awake.

Worrying about the secret cargo inside my suitcase kept me awake, too, even though I used it as the hardest, most uncomfortable pillow ever. I can't feel too sorry for myself, though. Papá, Emilio and Enrique didn't sleep at all, because they guarded the wagon, the burros and goats.

I cried when it came time to say goodbye. Even Papá teared up. I've shed more tears in the past month than I have in the past thirteen years combined. You'd think my body would have dried out and shriveled up by now, like an old apple.

"I miss Papá and Emilio already," Elsa sighs.

"Me, too," I add. "We won't see them for at least two weeks. Maybe we shouldn't have packed so many things. How are Félix and Felipe going to make it all that way pulling that much weight? What if one of them breaks a leg or something? How will Papá and Emilio get to Seneca? Will the goats even make it that far? Whose foolish idea was it to bring them with us anyway?"

I wipe the dirt from my hands on my skirt and chew the nail on my little finger.

"Evangelina, don't start. They're going to make it to Seneca just fine. All I was saying is I'm going to miss them," Elsa scolds.

"How did you girls sleep?" Enrique bumps his shoulder against mine. "I stayed awake, outside in the open air and did just fine. Who needs a tent, besides you weakling girls?"

"I do, but I'm just another weakling girl," Mamá answers. She walks up hand in hand with Domingo. "Too many mosquitoes without it. You know all about those right, m'ijo?"

"Yes, I do," Enrique says through his teeth as he scratches his neck, then his arm, then his shoulder.

"They got me everywhere! Even here!" He points to the seat of his pants.

Domingo doubles over with laughter. "That's the funniest thing I ever heard! Mosquito bites on your butt!"

"You wouldn't think it's so funny if *you* had itchy bites down there, you little rat!"

Enrique chases Domingo around the bench as he giggles and scrambles to hide behind Mamá's skirt.

"Serves you right for calling us girls weaklings, *m'ijo*," Mamá scolds.

We head inside the station and pass the time sitting along the wall farthest from the main entrance, eating two-day old *pan de dulce*, finishing the last of the grapefruit juice and playing *Lotería*. Mamá sits on the edge of a well-worn bench, a deck of cards in hand. Elsa, Enrique, Domingo and I sit at Mamá's feet, a rectangular card about the size of two stalks of corn laying side by side on the grimy floor in front of us, each card with a unique combination of sixteen pictures—four across and four down. My card has an umbrella, a watermelon, a devil, a musician, a spider, a star, a bonnet, a shrimp, a hand, a cactus, a ladder, a barrel, a parrot, a fish, a mandolin and a man with the world on his shoulders.

Mamá pulls a card out of the deck and announces, "It's the cactus."

Domingo and I each grab a dry pinto bean from a small sack between us and place it on our cards.

"¡Lotería!" Domingo yells.

"Did you get four in a row?" Elsa leans over and examines his card. "You sure did. Congratulations, you won!"

"I haven't won even once yet," Enrique protests. "The whole world is against me."

"Not me! I just won!" Domingo boasts.

"How wonderful for you," Enrique mocks.

"Maybe you have the weight of the world on your shoulders." I point at the picture on my card and try not to burst out laughing.

"Very funny," Enrique rolls his eyes.

The steady hum of the crowd picks up as more people enter the station. A man behind the ticket window opens up the pulldown shades and turns the hanging sign from "At Lunch" to "Open."

Travelers stand together like kernels of corn on a cob. A young woman about Francisca's age stands barefoot near the door. A checkered shawl drapes over her head and wraps around her body. A baby no more than a month old lays inside a fold in the fabric and cries as one little arm breaks free and flails around helplessly. The woman pays no attention. Three other small children cling to her skirt, all with dirty clothes and thin, listless and expressionless faces. Countless others look the same, weary and pale and so skinny their tattered clothes hang on them like scarecrows without straw.

"Can we share some of our bread?" Elsa asks, her face taut and stressed. "Some of these people are so thin. That old woman over there is begging for food."

"That's a very kind thought, Elsa. Here, take my bag." Mamá hands her woven bag to Elsa. "There are four or five *bolillos* in there. Why don't you tear each of them in half first?"

Elsa slings the bag over her shoulders so it hangs in front of her right hip. She tears the bread into pieces and within seconds a swarm of people leans in with outstretched hands.

"Please, señorita, have mercy on me. I haven't eaten in three days. Please."

"Señorita, my child is sick. If only she could eat a little of your bread."

"The hacienda owner fed us nothing but rice and water."

"Señorita, can you not see my baby is hungry? Please, I beg of you. God have mercy on you."

The rest of us cluster together, distressed at the sight. I've never gone hungry, but these poor souls . . . I can only imagine what they've been through.

Elsa hands bread to as many people as she can, but there are so many empty hands! In less than a minute the bread is gone, and the people scatter like crows when an eagle circles in the sky above.

"I'm sorry, it's all gone," Elsa apologizes to those who didn't get any. "Mamá, there's none left."

"I'm glad you shared what we had. Those people were much hungrier than we've ever been. We still have fruit and nuts, and a bag of dried meat," Mamá assures her.

"Enrique, come with me to the ticket window. They told your father we couldn't get our tickets more than an hour before departure," Mamá instructs. "It's ten o'clock, so it should be fine now." Mamá gestures toward the double-wide open doors. "Girls, take our things over there so they're closer to the platform. I don't want to fight the crowd when it's time to board. Keep Domingo with you, and don't let him out of your sight."

"How are we going to get it all over there?" Elsa huffs.

"We'll just have to manage," I grumble. "Let's take the suitcases, and I'll come back for Enrique's crate. Now come on."

I pick up my own light brown suitcase with the dark brown belt around it. My doll Belinda is wedged inside between clothing. I'm not leaving that bag behind. I stuff

Domingo's little suitcase under my arm and pick up Mamá's suitcase with my free hand. Elsa grabs her own and takes Domingo's hand. They trail behind me.

"I smell roasting corn. Maybe they're selling some outside. I'm still hungry," I say. "Do you smell it?"

No answer.

I wheel around to a sea of strange faces. "Elsa?" I call. "Elsa?" I try again, louder.

I make my way to the area Mamá directed us to, drop the suitcases against the wall, careful to place mine in the very back.

"Elsa, Domingo?" I shout as I wade toward the center of the room.

"Lina, over here," Elsa calls from the spot I just left next to the suitcases.

"Where were you? Don't scare me like that!"

"I'm sorry, Lina. Domingo saw a lady with a kitten, and we just had to stop. He was so tiny, just six weeks old. His name is Chacho. Isn't that cute?"

"Uh-huh. I need to go back and grab Enrique's crate. Wait here, and don't move."

I push through the crowd more aggressively this time, grab the crate and hustle back to Elsa and Domingo. Mamá and Enrique stand with them now.

"The next train to Paloma is leaving sooner than I thought." Mamá holds up the tickets. "I had to pay the man an extra ten pesos for us to get on. Many of the people here have been waiting for days, even weeks. There are so many trying to get to the United States, and there just isn't enough room—that is unless you hand the man an extra ten pesos." She smiles weakly.

Enrique shrugs. "Let's sit on the suitcases and wait. What else is there to do?"

I turn toward the spot where I left my suitcase. "My suitcase!" I yell. "Where is it?"

"Where did you put it down?" Mamá asks.

"Right here with all the others! It was right here against the wall. No, no, no, this can't be happening!"

"Maybe you set it somewhere else close by. You and Enrique, go look for it. We'll wait here for you," Mamá promises.

"Enrique, we have to find it!"

"What's the matter with you? You look pale," he exclaims.

"You don't understand. I have to get it back!" I can't let Abuelito down. What if the wrong people got a hold of it like he warned?

"Okay, fine. You go that way, and I'll go this way."

We head in opposite directions. My eyes dart back and forth.

"Has anyone seen a brown suitcase with a dark brown belt around it?"

Most people don't answer or even look my way. Others simply shake their heads. I force my way to the ticket counter and push up to the front of the line. People shake their fists and curse at me.

"What do you think you're doing?"

"You can't do that, young lady!"

"You little brat!"

"Señor? Señor?" I plead. "Has anyone turned in a brown suitcase with a dark brown belt?" The man behind the counter with narrow eyes, pockmarked skin and slicked-back hair screams at me.

"Get in line!" he bellows.

My mother waves me toward her. She, Enrique and Elsa grab our things and walk to the rail station double-wide door. A deafening whistle blasts from the oncoming train.

"Evangelina, hurry!" Mamá shouts. I get to the train just as its doors slide open.

"Come on. Let's find a seat quickly, before they all fill up," Mamá orders.

"Mamá! My suitcase . . . I can't leave it behind. Please, can I look for it just another minute?"

"Is your head filled with rocks?" Enrique spouts off. "The train is about to leave. Get on, now!"

I turn and scan the building one last time. So many people, but no suitcase, so I hop in.

"I lost it," I sob to no one in particular. "Where could it have gone? I know I set it down by the other ones. Someone took it!" My nose runs.

The train doors close, the whistle signals our departure. The railcar lurches forward, and we stumble forward.

I turn and whisper to Elsa. "That suitcase had something important in it."

"What?" she asks.

"I can't tell you," I whisper through trembling lips. "I promised I wouldn't."

"Here," she hands me her embroidered handkerchief. "I don't know what you're talking about, Lina, but I'm tired, and it'll be hours before we get there. I'm sure we'll be able to replace whatever was in that suitcase, or you'll have to live without it." She takes a deep breath. "All these people make me nervous. Let's find a place to sit and rest, all right?"

Chapter Eleven
Thief

May 31, 1911

The muggy air sticks to me like paint on wood. The conductor blows the whistle again, and the clickety-clack-clickety-clack rhythm picks up underneath us. I stand in a tight huddle with my family and look across the railcar. Packed wooden benches line the outside walls under the windows, most of which are cracked, broken or missing. Two thin, look-alike unshaven men sit next to each other. Bullet belts crisscross over their torsos. They don't strike me as dangerous, but they could have guns tucked away somewhere. I can't guess how old they are. Maybe twenty? The skin on their faces hangs loose over high cheekbones and pointy chins. Their dusty hair needs washing and combing. The man on the left has a bloody, bandaged hand. A cane rests against the knee of the man on the right.

A gray-haired man snores loudly next to them. His head sags over his chest, the corner of his mouth wet with drool. An empty beer bottle hangs from his limp hand.

One woman holds a crying baby over her shoulder and pats his back; another woman cradles two girls, a baby and a toddler. There's a gaping hole between the baby's upper lip and nose. One tiny tooth sticks out at an odd angle from her misshapen upper gums. Poor little thing. I've never seen that before. How will she ever eat?

A little boy sits with his ankles crossed and a mango-filled sombrero at his feet. He watches the mangos perhaps worried that someone will steal them?

Some people sit in seats, others cover the floor. Many pull their shoulders and legs in tightly to make room for others, or perhaps to keep from touching the person next to them. Suitcases, baskets and bags cover people's laps or rest between one person and the next.

"There's no room," Mamá says. "Let's move to the next railcar. Walk this way." Mamá moves a step to the left.

"I don't know how we can even get to the next railcar, it's so crowded," Enrique comments irritably.

"Do the best you can, and just say, 'excuse me.' This is going to be a long train ride. Do you want to stand here the whole time?" Mamá asks the question but uses her do-as-I-say voice.

"No . . . "

"Then do it," Mamá orders.

We search for small spaces to step into and lift our suitcases as high as we can so we don't knock into anyone. It takes a good five minutes to make our way to the end of the rail car. I push open the door, step onto a small wooden platform, breathe in the fresh air and walk up a few steps to the door on the other side. I pull it open, step in and suck in my breath.

"That's my suitcase," I tell my mother.

"Are you sure?" Mamá whispers. "And keep your voice down. We don't need any unwanted attention."

"Yes, that's it. See the belt around it?"

Relief and anger creep in and make my face hot. A young girl about my age is on top of my suitcase. She stares at me with innocent eyes, as if thinking, what could she be staring at? Her knee peeks through a hole in her frayed yellow and white polka dot dress. A gray shawl hangs over one shoulder and ties in a knot over the other so it drapes sideways across her chest. She sits cross-legged with a man's well-worn boots sticking out from under her dress. Long black hair hangs loosely around her face. One side of her hair is oddly shorter than the other. Scabs and purplish swollen skin cover one arm. I look away.

Enrique steps forward and noisily clears his throat. "Excuse me. That is my sister's suitcase. Give it back."

"No," she answers. "It's my brother's."

"That's MY suitcase," I burst in.

"Evangelina, I will handle this." Enrique pulls his shoulders back and tries to look taller. "Look, miss, you may think that's your brother's suitcase, but it's not. It's my sister's. I know because of the belt around it. Your brother must have picked it up accidentally, now give it back."

"No," she barks.

"Listen here!" Enrique demands. "You will do what . . . "

"Mamá, can I sit with her?" I interrupt my brother before he makes it worse. "We can just talk."

"That's a bad idea," Enrique scowls. "You should let me handle this."

"It's all right," Mamá says. "We'll stand right over here." She gestures in front of her to a small space against the wall. "You call me or your brother if you need to."

Mamá gives me a look of confidence. My mother and siblings find their way through the bodies and stand a few meters away. Enrique glares at the girl.

"Can I sit here with you?" I ask. "Next to the suitcase?"

"Yes, but it's not your suitcase," she says defiantly.

"What's your name?" I ask.

"Margarita," she responds. "Margarita Belén Delgado. What's yours?"

"Evangelina Carmen de León. I'm fourteen, or almost fourteen."

"I'm fifteen, but my birthday is in July."

"So is mine, on the first."

"Mine, too!" she grins, but it fades as quickly as it came. "I know you want this suitcase, but I can't let you have it. My brother said . . . he said . . . "

"Your brother said what?"

"To guard it."

"Did he say why you had to guard it? And, where is he anyway?"

"He didn't want anyone to steal it. There are thieves everywhere, you know. And, he's walking through the other railcars looking for something. He'll be back."

"Did he have the suitcase before you got to the train station?"

"Of course he did. . . . Or maybe he got the suitcase *at* the train station. I can't remember."

"Then it's mine, and you know it is. He stole it."

She stares straight ahead. Her cheek twitches.

Minutes go by before I try again. "I'm sorry about your arm," I say. "It looks like it hurts."

Her lower lip quivers and tears spill out as she slides her arm out from under her shawl to show me the purplish-red skin pitted with round ashy black spots and open sores. She wipes away her tears leaving smudges of dirt across her face.

"I don't have a brother," she confesses. "My parents and sister are dead. Please don't tell! I'm so hungry. I ate a corn cob from the garbage behind the train station," she says weakly. "I've been finding things . . . things to sell, like your suitcase. I'm sorry. I know it's sinful. It's not how my parents raised me."

I put my arm around her shoulder. "I'm very sorry," I offer. "We have food. I'm sure my mother won't mind sharing some."

My stomach flip-flops. It's been a while since we ate, and I'm hungry again.

"Would you?" she asks.

"Of course, but I can't let you have the suitcase. It has everything in it, at least everything I could take from our house. We had to leave our ranch because of the war. We're going to Texas to live with my aunt. I don't know if we'll ever go back home. But I hope we do."

"You lived on a ranch? Are you rich or did you work there?"

"We're not rich. At least I don't *think* of us as rich. We live right outside Mariposa at Rancho Encantado. It's been in my father's family for generations. Where did you live?"

"Hacienda Estrella near Rendón. But, not anymore."

Enrique comes back with an orange in each hand.

Margarita attempts a smile. "Thank you," she says, reaching out with her burned arm to grab the fruit, but instantly pulls it back under her shawl.

Enrique leans over. "Here, I'll give it to my sister, and she can give it to you when you're ready. I'm sorry it's not very much."

Surprise, surprise. My brother has a tender side.

"Thank you," she says with downcast eyes. "I feel bad taking your food."

"I'll set the food in my lap, and you can have some whenever you like," I say.

When is she going to give me my suitcase back? I wonder. Dear God, did she open the suitcase already and find the box? A sudden throbbing pounds my temples.

"Margarita, did you open the suitcase?" I hold my breath.

"No, I only took the suitcase fifteen minutes before we boarded the train."

"I was just wondering." The pressure in my head rushes downward. "Please excuse me," I say to Margarita as I stand up and move toward Mamá. "Do you have your Bible with you?" I ask.

"Of course, m'ija," she answers. "It's right here" she says, reaching into an outside pocket of the woven bag with the food and other small items for the trip. She unwraps a thin cloth from around the brown leather Bible and hands it to me.

I sit back down next to Margarita and open it.

"Do you know how to read?" she asks innocently.

"Of course," I reply. "Do you want to read it?"

"Oh, no, I don't know how to read."

My heart sinks. "Would you like me to read to you? We'll be here for a while."

Margarita nods.

"Genesis One. In the beginning, God created the heaven and the earth," I start.

She's asleep by page twenty.

Most of the travelers have settled in, and aside from the
a few conversations here and there and one fussy baby, the
only sound is the train barreling down the railway.

My resolve to stay awake fades, and I let myself float
into blackness.

*"Buenas noches, m'ijita. Come outside. It's a beautiful
evening, not too hot tonight. Do you see the colors
swirled together on the horizon over there? The sun was
on its way to bed and left those reds, pinks and purples
just for you, but they'll be gone soon. Why don't you sit
here so we can watch them together?" Abuelito pats the
space next to him on the top step of the front porch.*

*I stand on the other side of the screen door with my
nose pressing against the metal mesh. I smile, push the
door open, skip twice and flop down next to him. I wear
a blue and gray striped apron and a loose-fitting white
cotton dress. White knee socks gather in wrinkles
around the tops of my brown lace-up boots, worn at the
toes and dusty from playing outside. Abuelito's hands
rest, one hand on each bent knee. I reach over and place
my left hand on top of his wrinkly right one. "Abuelito,
what story will you tell me tonight?" I ask.*

*"Well, I don't know about any stories. I haven't gotten
a hug from you all day," he teases. "I know you just
turned six and that makes you a big girl. I know you
helped your Mamá in the house and picked vegetables
with your brothers, but that doesn't excuse you from giving an old man his daily hug."*

"I'm sorry."

*I pop up, wrap my arms around his neck and take in
the sweet smell of pipe tobacco on his shirt collar and in*

his thick hair, black and silver like the charred wood and ashes in the kitchen stove.

"Now will you tell me a story?" I ask as I twirl backwards a half circle and sit back down.

"How can I ever say no to such a smart and kind granddaughter? Not to mention one that has my good looks."

"Okay . . . but what about the story?" I tap his back gently to hurry him up.

"Have I ever told you the story about Gorgonio and the falling star?"

"Uh-huh. Gorgonio caught a star and took it home to his Mamá so she'd always have light in the kitchen to do her sewing."

"I guess I did tell you that one. Well then . . . have I ever told you how our little town Mariposa got its name?"

I tilt my head, close my eyes and sift through pictures in my mind of Abuelito's stories. "No, I've never heard that one."

"Well, it's an old story. I can't say if it's all true, but I like to believe it really happened."

"What happened?" I bounce up and down.

I scoot closer to him so our legs touch. A warm wind blows in and rustles the leaves on the trees. The crickets begin their nightly chorus of chirps, clicks and tweets. Mamá's pan de dulce bakes in the oven for the next day's breakfast. I close my eyes and try to taste it with my mind.

"Long, long ago," Abuelito starts, "a band of Spanish explorers journeyed from halfway across the world on a big ship in search of gold and precious stones. When they arrived in the New World, there were less than half of them left. Many died from starvation and scurvy during *the voyage. The surviving men arrived in a pitiful state, pale as that cloud over there, and wasted away to nothing but skin and bones. The men were weak, but they found strength and hope in their dreams of wealth and glory. They labored from sunup to sundown to uncover the riches they'd risked life and limb for, but found nothing of the sort, only natives who offered food, water and gifts. They decided to settle on the banks of the great river rather than go back to their king empty-handed. It didn't take long for them to marry the local women and build a small village they named Agua Fuerte.*

"It was there the people witnessed a magical event in the spring when God bestowed upon them earth's greatest bounties—splashes of color across the grasses, plentiful wild fruits, berries and abundant game. It was a time of beauty, a celebration of new life.

"One clear morning, thousands of butterflies appeared from the north. We see butterflies ourselves each spring, don't we? But this time, there were so many, they filled the sky in every direction."

I look up in wonder, hoping to see the butterflies myself.

"The outsides of their wings were lined in thick black stripes with white spots" he continues. "The insides were filled with orange, red and gold shapes that fit together perfectly like pieces of stained glass that reminded the explorers of the grand cathedral windows in the crowded city they used to call home. They fluttered in, out and around the great river. The people took it as a sign from God that, through the arrival of the butterflies, He was gracing them with His goodness and blessing all who lived there.

"But the next day, to everyone's surprise, swarms of pocket-size swallows dove in, out and around the great

river and snatched many of the butterflies for their meal. Some butterflies escaped. When the sun disappeared from view, the birds were gone, and the butterflies were no more."

"Ooohhh," I lament. "That's sad."

"It only seems sad, but you must hear the rest of the story." Abuelito put his arm around my shoulder. "Soon thereafter, the people of the village renamed Agua Fuerte, Mariposa in honor of the beautiful, noble creatures they believed God sent especially to them from up above to bless their village and all who lived there."

"Were the butterflies too scared to come back?"

"Naturally, they were scared of the birds, but they knew they could find a better place to live beyond what they could see, beyond what they'd ever seen in all their travels. And yes, they came through Mariposa the next year, and every year since then on their way to the warmer weather in the south," Abuelito replies. "The birds come, too, but that doesn't stop the butterflies. Fear doesn't determine their fate."

"What is fate?" I ask.

"Fate is the way your life is meant to turn out."

"Where does fate come from?"

"Fate comes from inside you," he says, touching my chest lightly with this fingertips. "Right here, in your heart."

"Really?" I look down at the spot where my heart is.

"Really! No one else decides it. It's what you choose, not something that happens by chance, like some people think. The butterflies know this, because they are wise creatures."

"Butterflies can't be wise," I giggle.

"Oh, yes, they can! Each one breaks free of its cocoon, flaps its wings, rises into the sky, travels long distances and overcomes many challenges and dangers along the way. But, in the end, it reaches its destination. It works that way for people, too, m'ija. Many small steps become long distances, with determination and hard work. You just have to know where you want to wind up."

I squeeze Abuelito's hand and lean into the warmth of his right side.

"Over the years Mariposa grew," he continues. "More and more families came to settle where the legendary butterflies first graced the great river, now called the Río Bravo."

"That's our river!" I proclaim.

"And just think . . . you were born here, on Rancho Encantado on the banks of the Río Bravo, right outside Mariposa. Evangelina Carmen de León was born July 1, 1897, and it was a very special day."

"You were born here, too," I remind him.

"Yes, of course," he agrees, drawing me closer. "But when you were born, it was a sign of God's goodness and grace, like the mariposas. God wants you to dream just as they did, then spread your wings, and go after your dream."

Chapter Twelve
A Different World

June 1, 1911

The sun is up, but just barely. I must have slept a long time. My neck hurts like someone folded it between the pages of a book. I hate when that happens. You fall asleep in a sitting position, and wake up with your head flopped over and slobber dribbling down your chin. I close my eyes and rub my neck. Images from my dream drift in and dissolve: Abuelito and me on the porch, looking to the sky for the butterflies, his arm around me. He always said dreams can foretell your future. That might be true, but he also said if you watched a dog poop, you'd get a sty in your eye. I told him that was the craziest thing I ever heard, but I admit I always looked away when I saw a dog squat. Why chance it?

Margarita looks out the window. With most of the window glass missing, there is nothing between us and the outside but a dirty wooden floor and a curved metal roof. The faint smell of orange blossoms wafts in. I hold my breath as long as I can. Our orchard back home is full of fruit right now, ripe for the picking.

Margarita holds out an orange slice with her good hand. "Do you want a piece?"

"Yes, thank you," I reply.

"I never told you the rest of the story," she offers.

"What do you mean?"

"What happened to my parents and sister."

"You don't have to if you don't want to."

Part of me wants to spare her the pain of reliving whatever happened, but part of me wants her to finish the story. She comes from a different world that intrigues me and makes me uncomfortable at the same time. There were so many people suffering while I lived an easy life on the ranch, without much thought to the world outside Mariposa.

"Señor Coronado owned Hacienda Estrella, all the land and the biggest house you've ever seen," she begins. "Over a hundred people worked there. Most of us worked the fields, or tended the animals, but some of the older girls got to work in the house, cleaning, cooking, running errands and taking care of his eight-year-old twins. Such spoiled girls and mean, too. My sister worked in the house. My parents and I picked cotton, and did other work, too. If I didn't fill at least two sacks as tall as I am, they'd whip me, just as they did the adults."

"How dreadful." I shake my head in disgust.

"My sister, Josefina, ran away, but they caught her."

"Why would she leave you and your parents?"

"She got beat almost every day by Señor Coronado's wife, who didn't like her cooking. She also didn't like how Josefina folded the clothes or polished the silver or braided the twins' hair. Señora Coronado used any excuse she could to scream at Josefina and whip her until she cried. That woman was an old drunk and mean as the devil. So Josefina ran away, but she didn't get very far. They dragged her back and whipped her so hard, she could barely move. Señora Coronado said Josefina would pay for trying to escape, but none of us imagined it would . . . turn out like it did."

I shift my position and let out the breath I've been holding.

"It was hot that night," she continues. "I asked Mamá if I could sleep by the door so I'd feel the breeze. That's the only reason I survived."

"What do you mean?"

"I saw him with an empty bottle of whiskey in his hand. He poured it on the hay outside our place before he set it on fire."

"Señor Coronado?"

She nods. "He was so drunk he could barely stand up."

She leans her head against me. Her tears soak my shoulder. I wriggle a bit to reach for the handkerchief in my pocket.

"Here, use this."

Mamá looks at me with an uneasy smile. I hold up my hand signaling her to stay where she is.

"People came running, shouting . . . the men brought buckets of water, but it was too late." Her thin frame shakes as she cries. "The next thing I remember is waking up in someone else's house, the house of an old woman who lived nearby. She took care of me for weeks, and then I just left. The old woman said Señor Coronado wanted me to get back to work, but I couldn't stay anywhere near that murderer. What was there to stay for? I'd rather starve than live there."

"Evangelina," Elsa calls from across the railcar. "Paloma is just ahead!"

I get up and stick my head out the window. The wind rushes past, loosens the hairs from the edges of my ponytail and whips them around and blows them into my mouth. A long, flat brick building with several arched doorways alongside a train platform comes into view. A giant clock hangs in the middle of the station's roof. It's seven o'clock. People mill about: men in sombreros, women with baskets and little ones clutching their mothers' hands. One little boy chases a dog down the platform away from the building. The whistle blows three times and a loud, lingering hiss comes from the engine up front as the train releases its last thrust of steam. The mist from the steam mixes with the warm air and rushes through the open windows.

People grab their belongings and jostle about as they make their way to the doors at each end of the car.

"Let's stay here while the others get off. There's no reason to rush. We'll be here for a while anyway," Mamá announces.

"Why are we stopping?" Domingo perks up. "Is this where Tía Cristina lives?"

"No, this is Paloma, but it's very close to Seneca, where your aunt lives. Paloma is still in Mexico and Seneca is in Texas."

"But I thought you said we were going to the United States." Domingo scrunches his eyebrows.

"Yes, Texas is a state *in* the United States."

"You said we're going to Seneca!"

"Ay, *m'ijo*," she sighs. "It's confusing, I know, but we have to stop here for a little while so some workers can check things on the train."

"What things?" Elsa asks.

She's been so quiet throughout all of this. When she gets nervous or scared or even excited, she stops talking. She thinks, then she talks. Sometimes I have to talk so I can think. Words come out of me like water from the spigot of our well. Enrique says words come out of my mouth like diarrhea. Yuck!

"Okay, everyone come closer," Mamá says. "Every train stops on the Mexican side before it crosses the international border, so that the Mexican inspectors can check the goods going out of the country. They'll probably go into the railcars, where the freight is stored and check what's in the crates and boxes. After this stop, we'll board one more time and cross into Texas, right across the river from Paloma, where we will also stop for a short while."

"Will they check *our* things?" Enrique questions.

"I don't know why they would," Mamá answers. "It would take too much time to search every passenger's bag."

I'm relieved. I wonder if they'd arrest us if they found the box. Why did Abuelito have to give me that stupid box? I'm scared of something I can't even name.

"When we get to the station across the river, if the Americans ask, we'll tell them we are going to visit your aunt in Seneca for a few weeks," Mamá continues. "Let's get off now. The next stop may be as quick as fifteen minutes from here, then about an hour into Seneca."

"Mamá, do you think Tía Cristina and Tío Mario will be upset when we get there?" I ask. "There *are* a lot of us."

Mamá pushes a loose strand of hair behind my ear. "Your Papá and I knew this might happen, so I sent her the letter a week ago . . . although she probably hasn't received it yet. If she doesn't have enough room, we'll figure something else out. Maybe the church can help or some other family will take us in. I was going to ask the church in town to help Margarita, too." She looks around. "Where's Margarita?"

I scan the railcar. No sight of her. But my suitcase is there!

"She must have had second thoughts about getting arrested for being a thief," Enrique says. "She's probably outside," he adds, like he knows everything.

We pick up the one item we each brought. It feels more than good to have my hands on my suitcase handle. Three steps down and we're on the train station platform.

"There she is! I see Margarita," I say.

Margarita stands at the street corner waiting for a horse and wagon to pass. I run to her before she crosses.

"Where are you going? I thought you were going to Seneca."

"Look at this!" she holds out a piece of paper. "What does it say, Evangelina?"

"Looking for girls to work as maids in the United States! Good pay! Ask for José Peña."

"A man told me they're looking for girls who can clean and cook and handed me this piece of paper. He said, 'José Peña is in that building over there.'" She points to a white brick building across the street. "Isn't it wonderful? I only just got here and already I have a chance at a job."

"Are you sure? You don't know any of these people, whoever this José is, or who you'd be working for. How do you know he won't turn out to be another Señor Coronado?"

"I can't miss this opportunity, Evangelina. I need the work. I've got to try." She grabs my shoulder and finally says, "I'm sorry about your suitcase. But I'm glad we got to talk. You were a very good listener. Thank you. I'll always consider you a friend."

She hugs me as best she can with one arm.

"Good luck, Margarita. I will pray for you. Make sure you get something to treat that arm!"

We eat all the food we have left and wander around to pass the time, but there isn't much to see. A man lets Elsa and me stroke his horse, a light brown dappled beauty with a golden mane. He calls her Olive and talks to her like a baby.

"How's my little beauty?" he says to her. "She's a beauty, don't you think, girls?"

Before he leaves, he gives us a sack of apples. "She's had her fill," he says, nodding to Olive. "Don't want her gaining too much weight. She's got a bad back."

Enrique picks up a stick as long as his arm and hits a rock with it off into the thicket of trees. Then he hits another rock and another and another.

"Did you see how far I hit that one?" he brags. "I bet it was thirty meters!"

Domingo sleeps on a bench just inside the doorway. Mamá sits beside him and wakes him up.

"Come on, *m'ijo*," she cajoles. "Time to get up. One more train ride, and we're there!"

"I want to go home," he complains while rubbing his eyes.

Tired little boy, protest and all, we board the train again. Elsa pulls Domingo gently along. His feet drag as if his ankles have cannon balls attached. He lets out a big yawn. Whenever I yawned without covering my mouth, Abuelito would say, "You're going to catch flies in there."

I hoist my suitcase up the step and into the train. It feels heavier every time I pick it up.

The back of the railcar has a few open seats. It looks like two people can fit there. Mamá takes one spot, and

Elsa takes the other with Domingo on her lap. Enrique and I stand. The train jolts and rolls forward.

"This may be the last time we're on Mexican land for a long time," I announce.

"You're right, *m'ija*," Mamá agrees. "This will be the first time any of us has traveled this far from home, much less left any of the fam . . . " She stops mid-sentence. Tears fill her tired eyes.

"We must trust in the Lord, and He will serve us well," Elsa says. "I pray for Tomás, Abuelito, Francisca and René every moment I get. And René's family, too. I'm sure you all do the same. Tomás is probably already getting better. I can see him now climbing trees and throwing rocks and eating something with more food on his face than in his mouth. You know, his usual self."

"Look!" Enrique calls out. "We're crossing the Río Bravo again. Halfway across this bridge and Mexico will be behind us."

"The Americans call it the Río Grande," Mamá adds.

Before long the steady thumping of the train wheels against the tracks slows down and stops for a quick check at Customs. "I don't see any tall buildings, just the inspection station," Enrique announces. "It's smaller than our house. I thought it would be . . . different. Bigger maybe and with some of those fancy cars I've seen in pictures."

"*M'ijo*, this is a small town," Mamá points out. "Maybe one day you'll see the tall buildings, but in a big city like New York. It's very impressive, or so I'm told."

I don't want to see a big city. I want to go home. But first, we have to make it past the Customs inspectors. I bite my thumbnail. I've kept my promise to Abuelito. The box is inside my doll, now in the United States. Now what should I do with it?

About half the people get off the train. The rest of us sit and wait.

Ten minutes later the train is waved on. Thank you, Lord!

The trip from the Customs station to Seneca is uneventful. I watch the surroundings as we roll past more small towns and huge tracts of land, some of it empty and lonely-looking. Eagles and hawks circle above fields of peach, pear, lemon and orange trees planted in rows at farm after farm. Cattle and sheep graze, windmills spin, carpets of wild daisies paint the ground yellow and white. It may not be quite as dry as Mexico, but still, much of it looks the same.

I doze off again and wake up to the sound of squealing wheels and the train whistle. The train stops, we gather our things and step outside. A chill runs up my spine, despite the warm, balmy weather. Less than a week ago I was making tamales. Watching Elsa try on her dress. Listening to Mamá go over the guest list. Celebrating Elsa's and Enrique's birthdays. Teasing Abuelito behind the house. Now, we're in the United States! Fear, excitement, nervousness and sadness fill every space inside my body. And relief, I suppose. I am relieved we're here, but don't want to be here. I bite my nails again, until the nailbed of my little finger bleeds. My hands are filthy. I don't care what Mamá says.

I trail behind my family as they walk away from the Seneca train station, which is more like a one-room house with a few benches outside covered by a long, angled wooden cover. If the size of the train station is any indication, this must be a tiny town.

We plod along with only an address as our guide. We don't know the town, so the address is meaningless. We make our way down a wide, tree-lined street. Elsa's hair lays flat against her head, her dress is wrinkled and dusty. She's normally such a neat, clean, proper person, but after everything we've been through, she's past the point of caring. Enrique's soggy shirt clings to his back. His suspenders hang down, one on each side of his hips. Mamá pulls Domingo behind her. The braid piled on top of Mamá's head sits at a precarious angle, like it might slide off.

"We need to ask someone about this address, 1918 Washington Street. I hope we're close," Mamá says wearily.

"Look down there!" Elsa calls out. "It's a store. Someone in there can give us directions."

"You're right," Mamá says. "Let's straighten up a bit before we go in. We need to make a good impression. This will be our first encounter with Americans."

Mamá undoes her bun and pins it back neatly on top of her head.

"Domingo, come here. Let me wipe your face. You look like you haven't had a bath in days. I suppose you *haven't* had a bath in days, now have you? We'll have to take care of that at your aunt's house."

She pulls out her handkerchief. Domingo stands still, his chin in the air. He's used to this. Mamá wipes his hands and face a lot. Dirt seems to grow on him. Normally, our clothes would be pressed, our shoes would be shined before we went into town, and there wouldn't be a hair out of place, especially for us girls. Today, we look, well . . . sloppy.

The store comes into view. "SENECA GROCERY & GIFTS." I recognize the word "Seneca." Shelves stacked with cans and boxes stand near the window. A large jar with wrapped candy sits on the counter. A woman in a white dress with a ruffled collar stands behind the counter and smiles at another woman, who turns and steps out the front door, hand in hand with a small light-haired boy about four years old. She stops and looks at us sternly for a moment, spins around, pulls the boy's hand and walks away briskly.

I turn back toward the store. The woman with the white dress stands behind the window and points to a sign at the bottom of the window sill. "No Dogs! No Negroes! No Mexicans! *No Perros! No Negros! No Mexicanos!*"

Mamá, Enrique and Elsa stare at the sign, then at the woman. Her pinched expression infuriates me. A strange sensation of tiny prickles starts at my neck and then flushes my face. Mamá grabs my hand and squeezes it.

"Let's go in," Domingo calls out as he pulls Mamá's other hand.

"Hold on, *m'ijo*," Mamá whispers.

"I cannot believe this," Enrique moans.

"What?" Domingo looks ahead, searching.

"Let's keep walking. The store is closed," Mamá says coolly.

"But I see a person in there!" Domingo cries out.

"Do as you're told," Enrique snaps.

"I saw bananas in there! Will the lady give me a banana?"

"No, *m'ijo*, just walk," Mamá commands. "We've got apples in my bag."

"I'm not hungry for apples," Domingo snivels. "I'm only hungry for bananas."

We walk faster now. We pass brick buildings with signs out front. I know the letters but not the words. J-DRAKE RESTAURANT & BAR. Schimke Bros. Farm & Feed. Zimbelman Tie & Timber Co. Large trees line the street. Green, yellow and orange leaves rustle in the wind. A gentle gust blows and more leaves fall, float, twist and spiral before they settle on the grass and sidewalk. A two-story white building comes into view with one door at the ground level. A staircase leads to the second level balcony and another door. An elderly man crouches on all fours and pulls weeds near the sidewalk.

We walk up and cast a shadow over the man, but he busily works away. His fingers look thick and curved, like my grandmother's before she died. He lifts his hat to wipe his brow with a handkerchief.

"*Buenas tardes*," calls the man as he pushes himself up. "Please let me introduce myself." He bows his head. "My name is Salvador Martínez. This is the local courthouse and school. I clean the place, tend the grounds and do anything else the place may need. The call me Mister Fix-it," he chuckles. "Is someone expecting you?" He motions toward our suitcases.

"Good evening, sir," Mamá responds. "We've been traveling for days, but I think we're almost to our destination, 1918 Washington Street, where my sister and her husband live."

"Well, that address is our little Catholic Church—an old house really. The Lord doesn't care where you worship so long as you do. Are you sure you have the right address?"

"Come to think of it, she said I could mail letters to that address. She didn't say she lived there. I just assumed," Mamá frowns. "She moved to Seneca with her husband three or four years ago. The name is Benavides . . . Mario and Cristina."

"I know Mario. Works for Texas Southern Railway. He's lucky. So many others can't find work except in the fields, and that kind of work comes and goes." The old man rubs his whiskers. "Most of us in town live on Washington Street, but it's not a real street like this one. Someone, probably an Anglo, named it after the first American president."

Elsa looks at me with raised eyebrows.

"If you want, I'll finish up and walk you to their place."

"We would appreciate that, Señor Martínez," Mamá says quietly. "But, I hate to trouble you."

"It's no trouble at all. It's my pleasure. If you would, please wait here while I put my tools away around back." He looks us over and rests his hand on his chin. "You must be hungry after a long day's travel. I'll bring you some corn bread. I have some inside. My wife tells me I get irritable when I'm hungry." The man shuffles off with his rake and shovel in hand.

"What do you think he means by 'it's not a real street'?" I wonder out loud.

"I'm not sure," Mamá says, frowning. "I guess we'll find out."

"Did he say he's bringing us something to eat"? Domingo squeals happily. "Because I don't want apples."

Chapter Thirteen
A Scruffy Bunch

June 1, 1911

Large front porches and thick green grass wrap around stunning homes, like in pictures from a book. Sweet smelling magnolia trees, rose bushes, neatly planted flower beds and perfectly shaped shrubs fill the yards around us. Our home in Mariposa has a large front porch, but no lawn, mostly tufts of grass with dirt and rocks in between.

"Do you think Tía Cristina's house will look like these? They're so beautiful. That one," I point to a giant yellow house with white shutters, "reminds me of a castle I saw in a book . . . with the rounded part and the cone-shaped roof, like there might be a princess hidden in there waiting for her prince."

"Evangelina," Mamá glances at me over her shoulder, "I don't know what your aunt's house will look like, but it won't look like that. But you're right about one thing. That is a beautiful house. The story you're remembering is Rapunzel. I read it to you when you were little."

"Oh, the princess with the long hair. I loved that book."

I picture myself as a small girl on Mamá's lap in the rocking chair, safe at home, leaning against her, covered up to my neck with a soft quilt.

"That was a stupid story. What girl would let someone pull themselves up on her hair?" Enrique teases.

"Well, I thought you boys didn't listen to princess stories. But from the sound of it, I guess *you* did!" Elsa retorts.

Suddenly, Enrique has nothing to say.

"The houses are much smaller here," Elsa comments as we make our way down the fourth block.

"We must be getting into the poorer section of town," Enrique adds. "Some of these people need to hire a carpenter."

"Keep your voice down, son," Mamá murmurs.

He's right. I see broken windows, rotting sideboards, peeling paint, a slanted house on posts with one post completely missing. Another house is boarded up. How could we go from such grand homes to such run-down ones in a matter of blocks?

"This way," our guide beckons. "Over the railroad tracks."

The light obscures the hand-painted wooden sign up ahead until we're standing right in front of it. Washington Street. We're here!

"It's only Mexicans here in this neighborhood," Señor Martínez clarifies. "A few very rich Mexican families live in town with the Anglos," he explains. "There's nothing fancy about our little community, but we can call it our own. I live here myself with my wife Patricia, just behind Amparo's *panadería*. That bakery has the best *conchas* in town. If you come to the little plaza just down there," he points down the narrow road, "after three o'clock on Saturdays, Amparo sells them at half price."

Up ahead, two barefoot boys in loose-fitting pants and shirts roll a wheel rim down the road with a stick and chase after it. A young girl about ten years old extends her arms to grab a chicken pecking the ground, but it runs off squawking and flapping. She sets off after it.

"Get back here you silly chicken!" she screams. She and the chicken get farther and farther apart.

The homes sit even closer together than the last ones, with only an arm's length between them. Some are little houses with just one room built of sandstone or wood. Others look like huts, *jacales*, made of sticks, rocks, mud, hay and palm fronds. Clotheslines run between them. Dresses, skirts, pants, socks, shirts and under things hang in the cool air. A few women unpin clothes and drop them into baskets before the evening dew sets in.

The homes end and shops begin. First is a butcher shop, *El Toro* Carnicería. Thick hooks hang above the display window with rings of chorizo, baby goats, chickens, slabs of ribs and haunches of venison.

Coronado's herb and spice shop sits on the corner with a painted door depicting a life-size Virgin of Guadalupe surrounded by heavenly rays. Across the street, empty bottles line the curb outside a cantina. A barefoot boy bends down to pick them up and sets them carefully in a sack.

"Señor, you've been with us for a while, and it's getting to be evening now. We don't mean to keep you," Mamá says. "Do you just want to point us toward the house? If you can tell us what it looks like, we can find it on our own. I'm sure you want to get home to your own family."

Señor Martínez points ahead. "Very good timing, seño-ra. Their place is there, with the aloe plant near the door."

"Oh, thank heavens! Thank you for your kindness. I hope we meet again sometime. You've been very helpful. We wouldn't have found it without you."

"My pleasure, señora. Perhaps I will see you and the family at church. I will introduce you to my lovely bride, Patricia."

"Thank you again, Señor Martínez! And may all be well with you! Come on kids. That's your tía's house!"

A few steps lead to a small porch where an aloe plant sits in a round planter etched with a palm tree design. Back home the aloe plants are large, some of them taller than three or four bales of hay stacked one on top of the other.

Home, home, home. I miss home.

Mamá sets down her suitcase, shakes out her hand and rubs her tired shoulder. The rest of us set our things down, too. Mamá walks up three creaky stairs. She pulls open the screen door.

Knock, knock, knock.

A soft light appears through the curtains in the front window. The door opens and Tía Cristina steps out. I remember her, but only vaguely. Her housedress hangs like a tent concealing a prize-winning pumpkin.

"Maríaelena!" Tía Cristina exclaims. "Why . . . how . . . ? What are you doing here?"

"Cristina, I am so happy to see you! And look at you! You are expecting another baby! I had no idea. Congratu-lations!"

Tía stands still, her mouth open and eyes as big as wal-nuts.

"Oh, I'm sorry to surprise you like this," Mamá gushes. "We left home nearly three days ago. I sent you a letter saying we might come, but I was afraid you wouldn't get it. Based on the look on your face, I guess you didn't. It's been a long trip. We're so glad to be here."

Tía's eyes scan across each of our faces. We must look like a scruffy bunch. She shakes her head slowly, tears pooling in the corners of her eyes. "You're all . . . so . . . grown up! Look at you! My goodness, why are you standing out there? I'm sorry . . . please . . . come in, come in!"

She steps aside, and we grab our things and step in the front door.

"Have a seat." She gestures toward the sofa and two wooden chairs. A child's rocking chair sits nearby. "I'll get you something to drink and eat."

She moves across the floor with the unmistakable gait of a woman heavy with child.

"I'll help you," Mamá offers. "You all stay here. I will be right back."

They walk through the doorway to what must be the kitchen. I lean forward and see the edge of a table and chair.

I find the sofa and sit down. Domingo snuggles up next to me and rests his head on my shoulder, thumb in his mouth. Elsa sits down in a chair, and Enrique shows himself around the house.

We made it! Sitting on a sofa in a room inside a house feels so good. It was only three days travel, but it feels like weeks. I want to sleep. I want to eat. I want to go home. I'm happy we're here. I want my father. I hope Tomás is doing better. I wish Abuelito was here. What's to become of us?

"Do you think she was happy to see us?" Elsa asks. "Do you think there will be enough room for us here?"

"I have it all figured out," Enrique says as he walks back in. "There's a big porch out back, all screened in. The men can sleep out there."

"So, not you," I giggle.

"I'm a man, you fool. If Elsa's old enough to be courted and get married, then that makes me a man. I'm in charge until Papá gets here. When it gets colder we'll just sleep in our clothes. That's if we're still here by then."

Mamá and Tía walk back into the room. Tía holds a tray with glasses of milk. She sets it down on the little round table in front of the sofa, walks to a cabinet near the front door and brings out a box of matches.

"Here, let me do that." Mamá steps over and reaches for the matchbox.

"Over there," Tía points to the candleholders on the wall, one on either side of the front door. "I'll be right back. I can't believe you're here!"

Mamá lifts the glass off the candle, strikes a match and the candlewicks flicker gold, orange and yellow. The light adds a softness to the room that only makes me more tired.

Tía comes back in with a plate of bread and cheese. Enrique leans over, picks up a large piece of cheese and pops it into his mouth.

Mamá frowns at Enrique and shakes her head. "*M'ijo,* why don't you offer your seat to your *very pregnant* Tía?"

Enrique stands and gestures toward his chair. "Of course. How rude of me. Tía, please, take my seat."

"Thank you. What a gentleman you are." She looks backward, grabs the back of the chair with one hand and steadies herself into the chair. "The last time I saw you,

you were this high." She lifts her hand to Enrique's waist. "All of you . . . you've all changed. Elsa, you are such a beauty. If I remember right, you just turned fifteen. I guess that means Enrique turned fifteen, too. You'll have to tell me about your *quinceañera* later. Evangelina, you're still just a tiny thing, but a young woman nonetheless. And that beautiful hair! I see a touch of red in it. I'm sure the boys have taken notice. And Domingo! What a sweet boy, look at him with all those dark curls. He looks like Adán." She locks eyes with Mamá. "Mario and I haven't had family around in so long. He found work with the railroad. That's where he is right now, working on the new line. I'm thankful for the work, but I've missed the family. I've missed seeing you all grow up."

"And what about Leticia?" Mama inquires. "She must be sleeping?"

"Yes, she goes to sleep around seven o'clock. She turned two a few days before Elsa and Enrique turned fifteen. We'll see how she does when her little brother or sister is born. "

"You must be due anytime." Mamá nods at Tía's midsection.

"Actually, I'm due in a month or two, or that's what the midwife says. I just feel so . . . big!"

"You most certainly are," Mamá agrees. "It must be a boy. Big and strong like his father."

"So, you will stay here? You're welcome here as long as you need a place to stay. It's a small house, just two bedrooms, but Leticia can sleep with us."

"Mamá and the girls can take the other room," Enrique adds, "and the men can sleep on the porch."

"Of course. There's no place to sleep out there now, so you'll have to make a bed with a few extra blankets I have in my closet. I'll see if the church has any straw mats and extra blankets tomorrow. I can't have you all sleeping on the ground out there."

Mamá puts her hand on Tía's shoulder. "This is so generous of you, Cristina. We showed up with no warning. The revolution was becoming too dangerous. The *villistas* wouldn't have hesitated to break down the doors, steal our things, take the boys or worse . . . the girls. We couldn't risk it. Adán and Emilio are crossing the border with the wagon and our things, or at least what we managed to load up. Francisca's husband René will try to sell the herd. Then we'll have enough money to find a place of our own."

"Will you settle in Texas permanently? I can't imagine you'd want to leave the ranch after all the years it's been in the family."

I hold my breath.

"We'll see. My hope is to go back to Mariposa when it's safe, when the fighting is over," Mamá says. "We had a good life there. And as you can see, Tomás is not with us, and he's not with Adán either. He's in Mariposa with Francisca. He was too ill to travel. He had a very bad reaction to a scorpion sting. When he is well enough, we'll go back for him. I pray it doesn't take too long. Francisca and René stayed behind to care for his mother and younger siblings. They'll keep an eye on Abuelito. All of them are staying in an old house René's uncle used to own, far from town."

"I'm sorry, Maríaelena," she says, reaching out and touching Mamá's hand. "You must be sick with worry, but you'll see them all before too long. I'm sure of it."

"Now eat, everyone!"

Mamá smiles brightly in the dimly lit room.

"Tía? Do you mind if I take my suitcase to the room where I'll be sleeping?" I ask.

"Of course, not," Tía answers. "It's the first room on the right. Leticia is on my bed, so the room's empty." She points down a narrow hallway.

The tiny room, the size of Mamá's and Papá's bathroom at home has an armoire but no other furniture. I stack my clothes and a few toiletries in a corner near the window. My doll, Belinda, stays inside the suitcase. I latch the buckles with a click-click, cinch the belt and slide the suitcase into the armoire, as far as it will go. Now what do I do?

Chapter Fourteen
Relief

June 21, 1911

It's been three weeks since we arrived at Tía's tiny house, which I'm sure was fine for Tía, Tío and Leticia, but with five extra people, we're bumping into each other. We're starting to get more and more frustrated with each other, too. Even Mamá's usual patience is getting tested. She's been short-tempered and worried about everyone at home, especially Tomás. We all are.

Tío Mario is nice, but quiet. He greets us in the morning and sits down with us at meals, but he's not good at conversation. Tía gets bigger by the day. She can't do too much anymore. I've taken to washing all the dishes, because her belly sticks out so far, her hands can't reach the sink. Without all my usual chores to do at home, I've done a lot more praying and asking for forgiveness for my sins, for leaving Tomás when I was supposed to protect him. Why is all this happening to us? I ask the Holy Father, but so far, He hasn't answered.

The neighbors are friendly. Most of them have come over to introduce themselves. I've wandered around the neighborhood and talked to people, but not very much. I stay at Tía's most of the time. I'm not feeling very social.

Besides, it's mostly boys around here, so Enrique has plenty of new friends. The few girls I've seen are much younger than me. Thank goodness for Elsa.

Enrique sets a pillowcase full of walnuts between us and produces a long nail from his pants pocket. We're so bored, we crack nuts to pass the time. The sun sits low in the eastern sky. It's only nine in the morning and already, the warm damp air has affixed the underside of our legs to the wooden bench. If it's anything like Mariposa in late June, it'll give way to choking heat by midday.

Enrique grabs an old cracked ceramic pot near the top step of the back porch and drags it over. "I'll open them with the nutcracker, and you pick them out with the nail. It'll be quicker that way." He goes back inside and returns with a kitchen towel he lays inside the dirty pot. "Put them in here."

"Helloooo?" a deep voice comes from the front of the house.

Papá!

Enrique and I spring up off the bench and practically trip over each other as we run inside. Elsa, Mamá and Domingo emerge from the bedroom.

"Papá!"

"Adán!"

"You made it!"

Our voices tumble together in a happy chorus.

Enrique slaps him on the shoulder and beams. "Where have you been, and why did it take you so long? We were starting to worry. I mean, the girls were starting to worry."

"It's a long story, *m'ijo*. I'll tell you all about the trip after we unload the wagon and clean up. I don't think I've ever been so filthy."

"We missed you!" Elsa says.

"We missed you, too," Papá says. "But there's no more reason to worry. We're here! It was a long trip, and . . . "

"Let me show you the house. I sleep back here," Domingo points down the hall. "I'll show you. Come on," he says, pulling Papá by the hand.

"Hold on there, m'ijo. We have to unpack. Will you help me?"

"Awww, can I show you later?" Domingo asks, undaunted. "I sleep with Elsa and Evangelina, but I want to sleep with the boys on the porch!"

"Of course, m'ijo. You can show me everything soon. Now, let me get a look at the rest of you."

Papá wraps one arm around Elsa's shoulders and his other arm around Mamá's. He leans in and whispers something in her ear. The most captivating smile I've seen since we left home spreads across her face.

"Thank you, Lord, for bringing them back to us," Mamá says as she fingers the rosary around her neck. "I don't know how much longer I could have waited. You can't know how relieved I am to see you." She shifts her gaze toward the front door. "Where's Emilio?"

"He got a job. Can you believe it? Such good news!"

"No!" Mamá turns pale.

"How could he get a job so soon?" Enrique asks.

"When we crossed the border, men crowded all around and offered us jobs—in the mines, the fields, the cannery, a brick factory. There were tables lined up right there to fill out paperwork. As many as twenty men who crossed around the same time we did boarded a train and headed off to work somewhere. That's what they wanted, right? To escape the war and find work. They were very fortunate."

"And what about Emilio?" Mamá twists the dishtowel in her hands.

"The New Mexico copper mines. The man said Emilio could make ten dollars a week. How about that? Ten dollars a week at his age, and the work came to him! One man next to us said he'd gladly take the job because he only made twelve cents a day when he worked on an hacienda near Mexico City."

"I only wish he could have come here first before he had to go," Mamá says. "I never imagined I wouldn't see him again."

"Of course, you'll see him again! I can't say when, but he'll get here eventually. He knew you'd be upset about this, but the offer was just too good. He'll send money every month. We're going to need it, Maríaelena. They tried to persuade me, too, but I'll get out tomorrow and start looking for work. There's bound to be something closer to home. I mean, somewhere in Seneca or nearby."

"How about me? I'm old enough and I'm strong, stronger than most fifteen-year-olds. Do you think they'd want me for the mines?" Enrique asks.

"Not yet, m'ijo, but your time will come soon enough. If your father finds work, I will need you at home," Mamá warns.

"I could go for just a . . . "

"That's enough, Enrique," Mamá scolds.

Enrique wants so desperately to grow up. As for me, sometimes there's nothing more I want than to stay a girl, even travel back in time to when I was seven or eight. Naive and untroubled with my family at our ranch on the river. Growing up feels complicated and stressful. Being an adult scares me, so I try not to think about it.

Tía Cristina steps out of her bedroom holding Leticia's hand and stops mid-stride. Both have wet hair from a bath.

"¡Hola, Adán! I thought I heard a man's voice! How are you?"

"I'm fine, thank you . . . " He says, looking down and gesturing toward his dusty clothes and shoes. " . . . a little tired and very dirty! I'm sorry we arrived unannounced and uninvited."

"I'm just happy to see you. It's been years." She shakes her head. "It's such a tragedy what's happening back home, but not much of a surprise. You're welcome here as long as you like. I'm sorry Mario is not here to greet you. He went to the *hierbería* to get some chamomile. As you can see, we're expecting a baby anytime, and I've had an upset stomach the past few days. He'll be back soon. He can help you with the wagon. Is it out in front? There isn't much room out there for a wagon."

"I left the wagon a few lots down in front of that empty barn, or at least I think it's empty. I don't know if we can hitch the animals there for long. Now that we're here, I can see it won't be practical to keep them. I'll see about selling them. There's a load of things that need to be stored, I'm afraid. Is there any place nearby . . . until we find our own place? Of course, you and Mario are welcome to use anything we have. We brought pots and pans, furniture, clothes, blankets, tools . . . you're welcome to it all. And may I offer my congratulations . . . on the baby, I mean."

"Papá?" I step out from behind Enrique. I can't wait any longer for my turn to hug him.

"Evangelina, my sweet girl. How are you? I didn't even see you behind your brother. I've missed you!" He says, wrapping his arms around me and squeezing tight. My head falls forward into the space between his arm and his side. I rock back and forth from one foot to the other, swaying with him gently.

"I've been having nightmares and praying for your safe return and . . . and . . . I'm just so glad you're here!" I wipe away the taste of salty tears.

"Let me see. Hmmm . . . you're as pretty as ever, but all those tears cloud your beautiful eyes." He pulls out a handkerchief from his back pocket, holds it up and grimaces. "I'd offer this to you, but I it's got a week's worth of grime on it. It practically stands up by itself."

"Adán, what have you been up to with that handkerchief? It looks like you dragged it behind you the whole time." Mamá takes it gingerly from Papá's hand and holds it by the corner as if it's covered with spiders.

"Oh, you know, normal man things like pulling roasted squirrels, prairie dogs, snakes and rats off a stick and things like that. It's been a hard trip. We were hungry and had many long nights guarding the wagon. Even had to fend off thieves who tried to take the mules in the middle of the night . . . but we managed. We're here!"

"Oh, Papá, you poor thing, that sounds awful!" Elsa exclaims.

"I'll wash it later, maybe more than once," Mamá says with a big grin on her face. "Let's go outside and unload a few things. Tonight, we'll celebrate your safe arrival."

Chapter Fifteen

Hopeless

July 1, 1911

I stand in someone else's front yard, on my birthday, in a town that doesn't seem to want me here. I ventured out beyond our little community once and smiled at a woman in a pretty pink house, but she didn't smile back. She went inside and shut the door. And then she shut the curtains. It's been a month since we arrived in Seneca, and nothing feels right. It's like a lifetime of wearing comfortable, worn-in clothes made especially for you, then having to live in someone else's too tight, too stiff and too scratchy clothes.

"I feel guilty living here," I tell Elsa. "There isn't enough food . . . Mamá and Papá hardly eat. Tía Cristina's going to have that baby any time now. I'm sure we're a burden."

Elsa adjusts her wide-brimmed hat to shield her eyes from the harsh sun. "Papá hopes René will sell the herd in Mariposa soon. Once that happens, we'll have enough money to buy our own house or rent one, since we may not have to be here very long," she says optimistically as she kicks the dirt with the tip of her lace-up boot.

"Papá said a man spit on him yesterday when he asked for work! These people think Mexicans are lazy and stupid!"

"Emilio got work right away." She twists a lock of her hair in her fingers. "He'll send money when he can." She looks away, but I see her wipe away a tear.

"We have to be honest about this. I don't know how we're going to survive here. Papá has asked about work at ten places in town, and no one will hire him. Some won't even shake his hand or close the door in his face. He left last night to go to the next town over in hopes someone there will have more kindness in their heart than in this insufferable place. Why do people in town glare at us so hatefully if they've never even met us? What would they do if the war was in Texas and their sons and daughters and fathers and sisters were being kidnapped and killed? Hmmm? What would they do?"

"Give it more time before you decide 'we won't survive here,'" she says, sniffling.

Elsa sits down cross-legged on a small patch of grass and picks a dandelion with a fluffy white top. She twirls it slowly between her fingers, tilts her head and admires its round perfection, then blows and watches the tiny puffs float, dip and turn like miniature dancers that disappear into the vast sky.

I shut my mouth. What else is there to say? No use in more complaining. I keep telling myself to stop, but I have a habit of saying what I think. It's a terrible fault of mine. I'll pray about it some more, but lately, it seems like the more I pray, the less God listens. For now, we'll just have to make the best of it with Tía Cristina and Tío Mario. She's my mother's only sister, but I only met her once before. She visited when I was five or six. We played with dolls, even though she was at least fifteen at the time. I'm sure she wanted to do something else, but she played with me anyway. I pretended she was a princess. Her shiny black hair fell to her waist and her skin was pale as rice. Her eyes were so black, the pupils melted into the darkness around them. She played guitar and sang. Her voice was like an angel's. I've even heard it in my dreams and imagined she'd sing at my wedding someday. I must ask if she'll sing for me again.

My stomach grumbles and interrupts my daydream. My last meal was yesterday's lunch. I skipped dinner— didn't feel like eating, plus there wasn't much food to start with. I look down at the large patches of dirt between the clumps of grass where tiny red ants scurry along cracks in the hardened ground.

"Papá mentioned school again. My English is not very good, but Tía has been practicing with me. I understand it better than I speak it. Same as you, Elsa. Do you think the Americans will laugh at me?"

Elsa puts her arm around my shoulders and pulls me close. "Of course not. Try to think positively. Let's go inside and see if Mamá and Tía Cristina need help in the kitchen. They're making *buñuelos* today."

"Good, because I'm starved!"

I follow Elsa up the porch steps.

"Do you smell them? They smell like *home.*" Her face brightens. "Hurry up, Evangelina."

My nose fills with the smell of the crispy, golden dough, all hot and sprinkled with cinnamon sugar.

"Hey, Elsa, you *are* coming to school with me, aren't you?"

"Evangelina, I need to find a job. Girls my age can work in Texas."

"Oh . . . I see. You go in. I'll be there soon." I fake a smile. "I have something I need to do."

Bad news on my birthday, on top of an already dismal situation. I've only had a tutor. I don't know what to expect at a real school, but I thought Elsa and I would figure it out together. This means Enrique won't be going to school either. Domingo is too young for school. So that leaves me. Once Tomás joins us, he'll probably start school, and we can walk together. I'll take care of him when he gets here—better than I ever did before.

"I'll take better care of you, Tomás," I declare to no one.

I head inside, eat *buñuelos* and rice pudding Mamá and Tía made special for my birthday. I thank them and make a wish to turn the clock back a year. That would be the best birthday gift of all.

———

I lie next to Elsa and Domingo, the three of us like logs tied together floating down a river. A hint of light filters through the old sheets nailed above the window to keep the dust and the mosquitoes out. I imagine it's five or six o'clock in the morning.

"Elsa! Elsa, get up!" Mamá cries out.

I jump out of bed, startled. I peek around the doorframe and see Mamá in the hallway. Her thick brown hair, pulled back with a scarf, hangs halfway down her back, her dark brown eyes look glossy and strange in the muddled light.

"Elsa is asleep. Mamá is everything . . . "

My eyes move away from her face to her wet nightgown and apron smeared with blood. I open my mouth, but my voice abandons me.

She grabs her shawl off the back of a living room chair, shoves it into my arms and throws the front door open.

"Your father and Enrique aren't back yet. I need you to go into town to the market plaza. You'll have to go on foot. There's a brick building next to the hat shop. Look for a green sign with white letters. It says 'Doctor Taylor' on it. Tell him to come immediately. It's an emergency."

"What is it?"

"Tía Cristina is in labor, and she's in trouble. Go quickly!"

I throw the shawl around my shoulders and lift my nightgown just enough to pull on my boots, pound down the steps, throw open the gate and run. I round the corner and a man in a horse and carriage approaches from the other direction.

"¡Ayúdenme!"

Oh, what's the word? What's the word? My brain spins. "Elp!" It finally comes to me.

The man slows his horse, stares at me, turns his gaze back to the road and continues on.

"Go on, Annabelle," he prompts his horse and passes me by. I pick up speed and fly down the road.

The market stalls, usually filled with boxes of colorful fruits and vegetables, displays of cowboy shirts, belts, fresh-baked pies, dried beans, books and confectionaries, sit empty. I whirl around looking for the doctor's office. In the pale morning light I make out the saloon, the barber shop and a ladies clothing store. There it is, next to the post office and hat shop. A small brick house with a green sign over the front steps: "Doctor Russell Taylor."

I pound on the door. No answer. I pound louder. "Elp, elp, plees!"

A twinkle of light appears through the narrow rectangular windows on each side of the door. A round woman with a long gray braid and white nightcap answers the door. She clenches her robe tightly in front.

"What on earth sends you here this early in the morning? The doctor's office is closed!"

"*Mi tía* . . . m . . . m . . . m . . . my . . . ant! Elp, plees!" I plead.

"We don't treat yer kine. Go fine one-a yer Mexican witch doctors to help you!" she commands, then closes the door.

I pound on the door again.

A muffled male voice rings out. The man's voice again, this time louder. The door opens a crack, and the old woman peers out. A tall blonde man pulls open the door.

"Hello, can I help you?" he says.

The old woman folds her arms, steps back and says, "Don't treat dem folks, son. People 'round here will be mighty angry with you."

"I'll take my chances. Now, young lady, what's wrong? Are you hurt?"

"Me ant ees . . . seek . . . mmmm . . . " I search for the word. "*Sangre*. Plees, señor, elp me!"

The doctor holds up his hand. "Hold on," he says turning and disappearing as the old woman stomps up the stairs.

He reemerges. "Can you tell me where to go?"

I nod and follow him around back. A sleek black horse stands in a tiny outbuilding with one stall. "Climb on ole Tilly here."

The doctor bends over and weaves his fingers together to make a step. I put my left foot in and swing my right leg up and over.

"Hold onto this." He says, handing me his bag.

In an instant, the doctor mounts and clicks his heels into Tilly's sides. "Yah!"

The horse gallops, and I point the way. Back down Culver Street, left at the tree with the white blossoms, right at the big yellow house with the fancy front porch, left again at the open field with the dilapidated barn and past the empty fruit stands alongside the road. We cross the railroad tracks into our neighborhood.

"¡Aquí!" I point at the house.

"Whoa, Tilly!" the doctor shouts.

He turns, grabs his bag from my outstretched hands, dismounts and runs up the porch steps. "Tie her up young lady, I can't have her wander off."

He slips in the front door.

I slide off the horse's side and tie the reins to a tree. I think that's what he wanted me to do. Did we get here in time?

I take one stair at a time, afraid of what I'll find inside. I tiptoe to Tía's and Tío's room, stand outside the bedroom and wait.

"I'm sorry, Missus ..." the doctor's voice trails off.

"Benavides," Mamá whispers. "Herr name ees Cristina Benavides."

He holds my aunt's hand and sets it down by her side.

"I'm sorry, Missus Benavides. I wish I could have been here sooner."

It's too late. I peer into the room. Tía Cristina sits on her bed with a tiny, still baby wrapped in a white cotton shirt. My beautiful tía who sings like an angel is silent.

Tío Mario holds their first baby in the crook of his left arm and stares vacantly ahead. Doctor Taylor stands at the foot of the bed, his black bag in hand, open and useless. Mamá leads me to the front room.

"*M'ijita*, Tía Cristina delivered a baby boy in the middle of the night, and all was well until about an hour later when the pains began again. Neither one of us knew there were two. I did my best to guide the second baby safely into this world, but it wasn't to be. He came out backwards."

"But why did he die?" I whisper.

"When a baby comes feet first it's difficult to get the head out." She pauses for a moment. "The cord was around his neck, and he couldn't breathe. God bless his sweet soul."

Back in the bedroom Doctor Taylor listens to Tía's chest with his stethoscope. Doctor Gonzales had one like that, too. The first baby now lies on the bed near his mother, swaddled in the blanket Mamá knitted in anticipation of his birth. His arms come loose and move around in tiny jerks. His cry is loud and desperate. Tío Mario leans across his wife, picks up his crying son and hands him to me.

"His name is Arturo, like my father, but we'll call him Tito. Take him so Tía and I can spend time with his brother." He looks at the second baby next to his wife. "His name is Jesús. He deserves a name, does he not? He is gone from this world, but God will love and cherish him in the next."

Tía's long black hair hangs in strings over her face. She picks up the lifeless bundle, extends her arms toward Tío and hands him his dead son. The baby looks perfect in every respect—a bit of dark hair, long lashes and a sweetheart mouth.

⁕

I sit cross-legged under the twisted old oak tree. Tito sleeps in the crook of my left arm. Ten tiny fingers, round cheeks and a wispy layer of soft black hair. I watch the ants bustle to and fro and flick the climbers off my dress. The United States is not a place of opportunity for all people. For foreigners, it's a land where people pass you by when you beg for help, hateful people close doors in your face and babies die.

I rock Tito gently back and forth in my arms, kiss his forehead and pray for a world where God's teachings of love and acceptance triumph over hate and divisiveness.

Doctor Taylor comes over to me and kneels down. He has golden hair with gray mixed in and crinkles at the corners of his blue-green eyes.

"He is beautiful, isn't he?" he says. "Made in God's image. You know you were brave to run into town and find me. What is your name?"

What is he asking?

His right hand touches his chest, "My name is Russell Taylor." Seconds pass. "I am Doctor Russell Taylor. . . . What is your name?" He points to me. "Your name, . . . is it, Dolores? Nora? Ida? Hilda?"

Oh! I understand now. "*Me llamo* . . . nem ees . . . Evangelina."

"Evangelina? That's a real pretty name. I am sorry my mother wasn't very nice to you. A lot of your people are coming to Seneca, maybe fifty in the past six months. People around here are just scared, afraid of what they don't know, afraid of change. My mother, she's decided all Mexicans are bad . . . anyone with dark skin, really, or an accent. Around here, a lot of folks agree with her. I don't agree . . . I don't agree at all. But you'll see, things will get better in time. You're brave, and I bet you're smart. I'll come back in a few days and check on your aunt and the baby . . . maybe in the evening, after I see my regular patients. Now, get some rest. You look mighty tired."

He stands up, strides over to Tilly, jumps on and rides off.

His words were a mystery, but his eyes were kind.

Chapter Sixteen

What You Make of It

July 3, 1911

"Evangelina, you will start school in August. You have a month to get used to the idea," Papá tells me after breakfast. "You'll learn math, history, literature, science . . . there's a whole world out there you don't know about, and this is your chance to discover it. There's only so much your mother and I can teach you."

I say nothing, do nothing. I mustn't give him the impression I want this.

"Sit down," he says, taking a seat at the end of the sofa and patting the spot next to him.

His dark, curly hair falls past his ears. It's longer than I've ever seen it before. The gray hair at his temples only showed up recently.

I sit down on the sofa next to him, and he wraps his arm around my shoulder.

"I've made a decision." He pulls his arm back, shifts in his seat to look at me directly, then crosses and uncrosses his arms. "And you don't have a choice."

"Can't Elsa go with me?" I plead.

"No, *m'ija*. Elsa will look for work to support the family. I wish it weren't true, but we need the money. Your aunt is not feeling well. You've seen how she is, and who can blame her? She's been in her room day and night. That means your mother is doing everything around the house and caring for Domingo, Leticia and Tito. She needs Elsa's help." He pauses. "Perhaps your sister will join you at school later," he says, but I know it's not true.

"I'm scared! My English . . . I barely understand it, and I can't say a full sentence, just words. How will I learn if I can't speak the language?"

"You'll do the best you can. What else can you do? Listen: When your mother went into town a few days ago, she spoke to Señor Martínez. He said he'd tell the teacher to expect you on the first day."

"Señor Martínez?"

"The man you met when you first got here. He showed you the way."

"Oh, yes, of course."

I try to remember what the school looked like when we first came to town. The courthouse and school share the same building. White, two stories, outside stairs to the second floor.

"Please, Papá. I'm not ready!" My fingers turn cold, and my stomach grumbles in protest.

"What is there to get ready? You will get dressed, your mother will fix you a lunch and you'll walk to school. The teacher's name is Señora Abbott. I'm sure she'll be a fine teacher. Listen, m'ija, the experience at the school will be what you make of it. All of us have to do things we're not comfortable with, and you are no different. Do you understand?"

He means that if it's not a good experience, I should pretend that it is. "Yes, Papá."

"Evangelina?" Mamá calls.

"I'm coming." I stand up, happy to end this conversation. "Will you excuse me, Papá?"

Mamá stands at in front of a grind stone on the kitchen table. A bucket of lime-soaked corn kernels sits at her feet.

"*M'ija*, your tía and tío's baby should have a proper burial with a wake and funeral services, but the house where they hold Mass can't be used anymore."

"Why not?"

"Someone left a campfire going outside. The brush near the building was dry. I'm sure it didn't take much for the fire to spread. So I plan to pay the funeral home in town for the use of the chapel. We'll do the wake the day after tomorrow, if the chapel is available. Mass will be the next day. I'll go to the funeral home in the morning and make arrangements. Will you go with me?"

Chapter Seventeen

Proper Burial

July 4, 1911

The white sign by the road reads, "Silver Family Funeral Home." Mamá and I begin our walk up the long, winding driveway. Lush green grass covers the hillside on both sides. We never had grass like this back at the ranch. It's very pretty, but who has time to take care of it? This place must not have any farm animals or crops to look after. Señor Martínez gave Mamá the address: 206 Leander Street. It's the only funeral home in the area. We found it with only one wrong turn. Señor Martínez's wife has lived in Texas a long time, so her English is very good. She wrote a note for us to give to the funeral director. We couldn't very well ask Tía Cristina to do it.

Between Mamá and me we can probably say twenty words, although we understand many more than that. We wouldn't even try to communicate with anyone about something like this. Señor Martínez started teaching me English, but we've only had four lessons so far.

We near the top of the driveway. A one story brick building with a white pointed roof sits at the top of the hill. Rectangular leaded glass windows with a crisscross diamond pattern flank each side of the front doors. Some diamonds are clear and others are creamy pink like the wild roses that spring up here and there around the ranch.

A covered walkway leads to a bigger brick building with three arched stained glass windows. Jesus fills the center window in his white robe, on his knees, hands clasped in prayer as he looks serenely to the sky where golden rays shine down from the heavens. The other long narrow windows are covered with yellow and pink diamonds in rows from top to bottom.

"We should be presentable before we go in." Mamá looks me over. "Straighten out your bonnet, and use your handkerchief to wipe the dirt off your boots. They're old, but they shouldn't look dirty. Now," she turns to her left and then to her right. "How do I look?"

Mamá adjusts the black and white plaid hat she found in Tía's closet. Three small black fabric-covered buttons stack one on top of the other to decorate the front and a lovely white bow ties around it at the bottom near the brim. Mamá's dress is pretty: black, buttoned tight at the waist, high collar and perfectly pressed pleats in the full skirt. A thin strip of scalloped white lace decorates the edge of the skirt near the hem.

"You look nice. Now let's go in," I say, smiling.

She fidgets with her hat again and takes a deep breath.

"Smile, and use your best manners. I don't know how they do things around here, so just be as polite as possible, and don't forget to smile."

I knock on the front door.

The front door opens. "Hello, can I help you?" asks a large, big bellied man with short, dark wiry hair and a dark suit.

I smile at him brightly to make a good first impression.

"Hola, señor . . . " Mamá says as she holds out the paper.

The man steps back. He puckers his lips and looks us up and down. He talks firmly, shakes his head and points down the hill. All I can catch is "Seneca," "no" and "Mexicans." He says "Mexicans" a few times.

"*Por favor,* señor," Mamá pushes him the note again.

He grabs it, takes one look and thrusts it back at her.

She takes the paper and hands it to me. "*Tengo dinero,* señor." She pulls her wedding ring off and displays it on her open palm. "*Voy a venderlo,*" she offers.

He starts to shut the door.

A young girl's voice rings out from behind. "Daddy, see my new dress for the Independence Day parade?"

She pushes in front of the man. Her yellow hair is curled and held to one side with a satin ribbon. Her bright red dress with a blue sash and shiny white shoes look like something from a book.

She points at us. "Who are these people? What nerve! We don't serve foreigners here!" She scowls. "Look at those ugly boots! What girl wears boots with a dress?"

The man pulls her in and shuts the door.

Mamá crosses her arms in front of her chest. "What . . . what was that? That man won't serve us because we're Mexicans? Is that what he said? He should show compassion. Especially in his line of work! What a monster!" An angry pink creeps up her neck and into her face.

My mind swirls. The man, the girl, no Mexicans, the dead baby named Jesús.

"The note said I would pay! I wasn't asking for charity. I planned to sell my wedding ring. It would have more than covered the cost. . . . "

I pull her away gently. "Let's go home. I wish we never came to this horrible place." She probably thinks I mean the funeral home.

The door creaks open again. The girl sticks her head out and watches us until we're out of view.

⎯⎯⎯

My mind skips around: school, Abuelito's box that thankfully has gone undiscovered, the girl at the funeral home, Tomás, my life, my disaster of a life. At home, the people around us loved us, treated us like family, even people we just met. Why are we being treated like this? Why do people hate us? We love and fear God, we're hard workers and we're only here because it was the only place we could go.

Elsa sits on the sofa with Tito, wrapped in a light blue blanket asleep in her arms.

"How did it go?" Elsa asks.

The tip of her little finger rests upside down in Tito's mouth for him to suck on. His long eyelashes flutter open and close again. Mamá hangs her hat on the rack by the front door. I pull my bonnet off and toss it onto a chair.

"We went to the funeral home to see about services for the baby. I offered to pay, but the man turned us down," Mamá responds flatly.

"What do you mean 'turned you' . . . "

"Maríaelena?" Tía Cristina asks, coming in, pale and thin like a strip of white gauze. "What did you say about a funeral home? Mario said there would be a funeral in town. I won't be going. You know I'm not well."

"No, no, no . . . no funeral home," Mamá assures her. "We will host the wake here at the house. Between outside and inside there's enough room. Everyone will bring food, and Father Miguel will say Mass here."

Mamá lifts Tía's chin gently to look directly into her watery eyes. "Listen to me. I know you're feeling very low, and no one faults you for that. You've suffered a terrible loss, but you have to face the truth and be a part of this . . . to honor him. You had two sons and one is gone, but one son is still here." She looks toward the baby. "You have a beautiful son who needs you. And Leticia needs you, too. I can only keep her away from you for so long. She misses her mother. Come on. Let's go into the bedroom. I'll bring you some warm water for the bath and make you cinnamon tea with honey. You clean up, I'll brush your hair, and you can spend some time with your children. I will help you, but you have to be a mother again."

Tía looks at the baby stirring in Elsa's arms, buries her face in her hands and sobs. Mamá hugs her and pulls her tight.

"It's okay to cry, Cristina. . . . " Mamá whispers softly.

Tía turns and disappears into her room.

Chapter Eighteen

Doctor Taylor

July 10, 1911

It's 10:30 in the morning. Iridescent lines float and squiggle above the puddles from last night's rain as the heat evaporates the water. Doctor Taylor arrived twenty minutes ago to check on Tía Cristina and the baby. He emerges from the front door and tips his hat.

"Mother and baby are doing fine," the doctor reports.

He's smiling so Tía must be okay. She still doesn't talk much, but at least she made it to the service and the wake. She's feeding Tito regularly now and letting him sleep with her. Tío Mario made himself a bed on the floor so Leticia can sleep next to her mother, too.

"Evangelina? That's your name, right?" Doctor Taylor asks, removing his hat and holding it at his side. "I have a note for you. I had my friend in town write it in Spanish for me. Name's Armando Hidalgo. Do you know him?" He shakes his head. "Ah! It's no matter if you know him. He moved here twenty years ago as a young man. Started a horse-shoeing business. Sells things on the side, too . . . saddles, harnesses, whips, used wagon parts and the like. Here," he holds out a letter.

I stand up, brush off the back of my dress and take the folded paper. It's in Spanish!

Evangelina,

My name is Russell Taylor. I am the only doctor in Seneca. There were two of us, but Doctor Gentry passed away about 6 months ago. It was sudden. I live with my mother Matilda. You met her the other day. She's not as friendly as she used to be, but she's 75 and loses her patience more easily now. She's having a lot of trouble remembering things too. I apologize for how she treated you. Even 5 years ago I don't think she would have talked to you that way.

I am a widower. My wife Susanna died in childbirth fourteen years ago. I lost her and the baby and never remarried. Since my mother is getting on in years she can't help me out at home like she used to. I'm busier than ever with my medical practice and could use some light house cleaning and maybe even a little help with meals. Would you be willing to work for me? I understand if you're in school and too busy for it. But, if you can come for just a few days a week, a few hours at a time I would be very grateful. I'll pay 20 cents each time you come. If you do a good job, I will make it 30.

You know where I live. My medical practice is downstairs. It's the same home my daddy built 30 years ago. I usually take lunch between 12 and 12:30 and finish up for the day around 6 pm. Please let me know your decision.

Sincerely,
Doctor Russell Taylor

Doctor Taylor doesn't look or dress like anyone else I know. He has light slicked-back hair with a little gray at the temples, blue-green eyes, a thin mustache, round glasses, shiny black shoes and a dark blue suit with a red and blue striped bow tie. His outfit is much more formal than the jeans, shirt, suspenders and cowboy boots Papá wears.

"*Tengo que preguntarle a mi padre*," I say.

"I hope that's a yes," he answers back as he hoists himself up and over Tilly, lifts his hat, tips his chin and rides off.

———

Papá stands by the front window and rubs the stubble on his chin.

"He wants me to work at his house," I say nervously.

"I see that," Papá says, glancing the letter again. "I don't know if I'm comfortable with this, Evangelina. How can we tell if he's an honorable man?"

"Well, he must be trustworthy to be the town doctor. And . . . his mother lives there."

"Did you agree?"

"Of course not," I assure him. "I said I'd ask you for permission. Of course, that was in Spanish, but he tipped his hat before he rode off."

"You'll be in school soon."

"I can work on Saturdays and maybe one day after school. I promise I won't let it interfere with my studies. Maybe he can help me with my English," I add hopefully.

"*M'ija*, the man is a doctor with important work to do. I don't imagine he'll have time to help you practice your English."

"I want to help," I plead.

"Help who?"

"Money, I want to make some money so we can move out of Tía's house."

"You are a very thoughtful girl, and I appreciate your offer. Maybe you can keep half and contribute half to our little savings. Does that sound fair? I got an offer to work at the brick factory in the next town over. They pay fifty cents a day, which is absolutely pitiful, but it's the only offer I've gotten. Your little bit plus my little bit plus what Emilio can send from his job in New Mexico . . . it'll add up."

"Does that mean I can do it?"

"Your mother asked Enrique to start going into town to sell bread and *empanadas* and anything else she has time to make. If he accompanies you, I'll agree to this. He can sell nearby and make sure you get home safely."

Chapter Nineteen
Ideal American

August 7, 1911

I've only been outside for two minutes and already my dress is sticking to me. It was almost as bad inside. Hot and damp is my least favorite combination of weather, especially on my first day of school when I want to look my best. Maybe there will be boys my age there. Handsome boys. Mamá finished my cream colored dress with the red sash last night with fabric left over from a quilt Tía Cristina made before the baby . . . babies were born. A braid on each side of my head coils into two buns that cover the tops of my ears, which is good. I've always thought my ears were too big, mostly because Enrique makes fun of them. Will I be dressed like the other kids? My boots are worn, but everything else looks nice.

A tortilla wrapped in brown paper fills one pocket and a pear fills the other. The one with the pear bulges out, but where else can I put it? Mamá said she'd make me a lunch sack soon.

"I still wish you were going to school with me, not just walking me to the school," I say to Elsa as we round the corner hand in hand. I see the Seneca Courthouse and

School up ahead. "My stomach hurts," I announce and bend over a little at the middle.

"You'll do fine, and you look very pretty," Elsa says and smiles.

"You're the one that turns heads, not me." I press my hand into my stomach to calm it down.

"Don't say that." Elsa blushes.

"I hope no one thinks I'm eight years old or something!"

"That's crazy. Why would they think that?"

"Isn't it obvious?" I roll my eyes.

"Well, you may be short, but you look like a fourteen year old in every other way, maybe even fifteen!"

"Can I practice my English with you?" I clear my throat. "Mee nehm ees Evangelina. Whas yorss? Orr how bout, watt thime ees eet?"

"That sounds good!" Elsa clasps her hands in amazement as if I just recited the Book of Genesis in English. "The lessons with Señora Martínez have really helped. You've picked it up better than the rest of us."

"I have to. I'm going into that school in a minute! You think the teacher will speak Spanish?"

"There's a better chance you'll sprout wings and fly. But there might be other Mexican students. We can't be the only ones in town who are sending their children to school, although I have to admit I haven't met any. With the revolution getting worse, more Mexicans come to the neighborhood every week."

Elsa puts her arm around my shoulder and starts walking again. We stare at the school just across the street. Horses and buggies line up alongside the building. A man in a fancy long coat and top hat walks by. A gray-haired woman exits a fancy carriage. Her driver ties up the dappled gray horse as she saunters inside the first floor door, her lacy pink parasol by her side.

I crinkle my nose. "Who are those people?"

"The bottom of the building is a courthouse. Señor Martínez said that when we first walked into town."

"Oh, yes, I remember. It will be interesting going to school in a courthouse. Maybe they'll teach us something about the law!"

"You're smart enough, that's for sure. I'm proud of you. I must tell Mamá and Papá how brave you're being."

A band of children runs out from behind the building, whooping and hollering as they tag each other. A girl with yellow ringlets points at us, and one by one the rest of the children stop in place. The happy voices and laughter become an unsettling stillness.

One boy sits by himself on the lowest step leading up to the front door. He jumps up and runs toward us, thankfully breaking up the standstill.

"Hello. How are you?" he asks in Spanish.

He wears shorts, a striped shirt with suspenders, a bandana around his neck and a brimmed straw hat. The other kids gawk at us.

"We're fine, thank you. My name is Elsa. This is my sister Evangelina, who will go to school here. What is your name?"

"My name is Alfonso Antonio Coronado. Come with me, Evangelina. I will show you everything. Do you want to come, Elsa?"

"My sister needs to go home," I say, swallowing hard and grabbing Elsa's hand. I squeeze it tight. "Good bye. Wish me luck!"

"You don't need luck." She squeezes my hand back and lets it go.

I turn to face the school. The kids go back to chasing each other around, but the girl with the yellow hair stands firm, hands on her hips.

"You new in town?" Alfonso asks as he grabs my hand and pulls me behind him. He must be ten or eleven years old.

"Yes, we've been here a few months only," I say. "Where are you taking me?"

"To see the school, silly," he giggles.

The hands-on-her-hips girl pulls a boy aside and whispers in his ear. He's as tall as Enrique and must weigh as much as Papá.

"Over here." Alfonso pulls me past the group of children.

The tall boy takes two steps towards us and spits at Alfonso, who jumps back just far enough to avoid getting it on his shirt.

"Sometimes they spit at me." Alfonso moves along unfazed.

"They?"

"Lots of boys and girls here don't like us Mexicans. The call us 'lazy' and 'dirty' and things like that. But don't feel too bad, it's only the boys who spit at us. They don't like foreigners, not just the Mexicans and the Negros. Only, they hate us worse."

Every bit of excitement I felt ten minutes ago evaporates.

"Where is the outhouse, Alfonso? I don't feel well."

"Sure, right behind the building, but you can't use it."

"Why not?"

"The teacher says if we go where the Anglos go, they'll get our germs."

"So where do I go?" I start to panic.

"Out in those woods, silly! Where else?"

"I can't do that." Sweat breaks out on my forehead and upper lip.

"Well, it's the woods or nothing. Or, you can hold it all day."

"I'll hold it," I say meekly.

"Here, come up here." He bounds up a few steps and motions for me to follow him up the long staircase. "The classroom is up there. I'll show you that first, but the room the other lady teaches us in is downstairs. I'll show you that later. I better take my hat off before Missus Abbott sees me. She gets real mad." He shrugs his shoulders. "I guess it's not proper. They're trying to teach us some manners."

We get to the top of the stairs. I peer inside the large white room. No one there, just long wooden tables with four chairs at each one, a large desk near the front and a blackboard longer than two men lying end to end.

"I'm glad you speak Spanish. Do the other Mexican kids speak Spanish at school? My English is terrible, but a lady we know is teaching me."

"Oh no, you must never speak Spanish where Missus Abbott can hear you, or any of the other adults here. You'll get in trouble."

"Trouble?"

He pulls off his hat and scratches his head. "I spoke Spanish on my first day. I didn't know English either, but now I do, of course. Lived here over a year. Anyway, me and Jorge got a whipping in front of everybody. Missus Abbott called Judge O'Leary from downstairs to come up and do it . . . in his long black robes and everything. Used a board with holes drilled into it. Called it the Board of Education. He made us stand with our noses touching that wall for the rest of the day," he says, pointing to a spot next to the bank of windows. "Didn't let us eat or go out into the woods or nothin', if you know what I mean. I nearly wet my pants."

"Alfonso? Why are you in here?" A shrill voice rings out. "Class doesn't start for another ten minutes."

The woman in the doorway is broad as a horse's behind. Her long black dress falls in pleats under the belt cinched tightly around her thick middle. A section of smaller pleats starts on top of the sash and runs up the center of the bodice where it meets with a button-up black collar. A white net holds her giant gray bun in place on her head. Her eyes are small as beans and dark as a raven.

"And who are you?" she demands.

"Mee nehm ees, ees . . . Mee nehm. ¡Ay Dios mío!"

I clutch my stomach, run out of the room, down the stairs, behind the building and throw up behind a bush. Oh dear God, what have I done? What have I done? Grab some leaves and cover it up! I look around. No leaves.

"Evangelina! Where are you? It's Alfonso."

I wipe my mouth with the back of my hand and run out from behind the bush. Smile, smile, it'll be okay. Elsa said I'm brave. Be brave!

"Oh. I see you found the Mexican outhouse." He grins at me sheepishly. "If you want to do the big stuff, there's more bushes further out. Come on. I told Missus Abbott you're the new girl. I told her your name, too. Your first name that is. What is your last name anyway?"

"de León," I say. Pretend like nothing happened, pretend like nothing happened.

"Oh, you'll want to tell her that when you get inside. She needs to know your name and age. She might ask you more stuff, too. I can help translate if you need me to."

"Fourteen," I say. "I turned fourteen in July." At least my stomach feels better.

"Oh, you'll be one of the oldest ones. There are lots of girls in the class your age. But there's one you should stay away from. Rosemary. You saw her. She's the one with the fancy blonde hair. She's not very nice to us Mexicans. She's sneaky, too. She made Victor put a dead rat in my lunch bag. Scared me so bad I cried, and everybody made fun of me. I'm ten now, so I wouldn't cry anymore. I'm braver now than I was when I was nine."

"Is the girl, Rosemary, the daughter of the man from the funeral home?"

"Her father is someone important in town. She brags about it all the time. Brags about all their money, too. Now, come on. Class will start any minute." He starts up the staircase again and turns back. "I almost forgot. There's another kid your age. He may even be older than you. His name is Selim, from Leb, Leb . . . some country even farther away than Mexico. Back up the stairs we go. I bet the rest of the kids are already in there."

I look up the stairs and let out a deep breath.

"You know you have to come up here if you want to go to school, right?" Alfonso waves me up.

I step inside the classroom. All the children face forward in their chairs at the long tables. A small chalkboard and piece of chalk is on the table in front of each student.

Alfonso announces something: I hear my name. I can understand that much. The children turn around. Missus Abbott frowns, says something sharp and points to an empty chair behind the table closest to the door.

"Sit here," Alfonso pulls out the chair for me to sit. His chair is next to mine. The two Negro girls sit next to him. A dark-haired boy smiles at me from the end seat, says something and slides his chalkboard and chalk toward me.

"He says you can use it until you get one," Alfonso tells me. I nod to the older boy and gulp.

———

"So how did it go, *m'ija?* Tell me all about it!" Mamá says, sitting me down on the sofa and patting my leg. "Did you enjoy it? How was the teacher? What did you learn?"

"The day went so quickly."

"What is your teacher's name?"

"Missus Abbott. She seems mean, but I didn't understand much of what she said, anyway. She's strict and never smiles."

"What did she say to you?"

"She didn't say too much to me, but there was a boy named Alfonso. He's knows English, so he translated for me. There are other Mexican children, all younger than me: three boys, including Alfonso, and two girls, seven or eight years old.

"There's an older boy. I don't know where he's from." My breath catches in my throat as I think of the older boy's handsome face. "And two Negro girls . . . sisters, I think, or maybe even twins. We all got sent downstairs to another classroom in the afternoon, but not the Anglo kids."

"Why was that?"

"Alfonso said we had to go downstairs and get lessons from a lady named Missus Clayton. She talked a lot, but I didn't understand her much, just a few words and some numbers. That's all I can remember. She sent us out to play after lunch, talked at us some more, then gave me a letter to bring home."

"Did you read it?"

"No, I didn't think I was supposed to read it. It's for you."

"All right, let me see it."

Mamá takes the letter and pulls a sheet of paper out of the envelope.

"Well that's a surprise, it's written in Spanish. I'll read it to you."

This letter is for the mother of the foreign-born child or children in your household. Your son or daughter is now attending Seneca School in Cutler County, Texas. As a good Christian and servant of the Lord, I have been asked to teach your child how to become an ideal American.

I, along with the other good women of Seneca, want you and your child to learn important lessons which will be more in line with traditional customs and foster greater respect for our law-abiding country.

First, let me say that I am encouraged by what I've experienced so far with the other foreign women and children with whom I've been asked to train, and it is my pleasure to do so. Your son or daughter will be learning things like how to set a table and serve food, how to dress properly and attend to basic hygiene, as unsanitariness will not be tolerated. As we all know, that can spread disease. Our collective health is of utmost importance as I'm sure you'll agree.

This will require patience on my part to be sure, as I know you come from a country with very different habits. But if we work together as Christians for the good of the community and America at large, I'm sure we will all be proud when you learn and apply the essential things you need to be valued here and help us solve the social problems that come with so many foreigners crossing our borders.

Once the first lessons are complete, we will move to the decorative arts, as the foreign-born mind expresses itself best through activities rather than abstractions, such as arithmetic or science.

I look forward to the progress that is sure to come. I also offer my services should you want me to come to your home and impart these lessons on other members of your household. May God bless.

Sincerely,
Mrs. Richard Clayton

Mamá drops the letter.

Chapter Twenty
Hard to Believe

August 14, 1911

It's five in the morning, and I sit alone at the kitchen table, ankles crossed, mindlessly sorting a mound of pinto beans into two piles; in one pile—cream colored beans with little brown spots and in the other pile—shriveled black beans, tiny pebbles and clumps of dirt. The tick tock rhythm of the clock in the next room keeps me company. A door opens and closes down the hall. The wood floors creak noisily under someone's feet.

Papá walks in and puts a hand on my shoulder.

"*Buenos días,*" I whisper.

"Evangelina, will you please come with me?"

I can't read the expression on his face. Am I in trouble?

"Tía asked me to sort the beans. They have to be washed and put in to soak before I go to school."

"Let's go outside."

We sit on a bench under a loquat tree in the backyard. Tiny, round, bright orange loquats in various stages of decay dot the grass. Normally, I would pick up one of the good ones and pop it into my mouth, but right now, the last thing I want is something to eat. I sit down beside Papá.

"I received a letter today from your Abuelito," he begins.

My heart thumps, then speeds up.

"The letter was hand-delivered by an acquaintance from Mariposa, Máximo Flores. Do you remember him?"

"Of course, he's Señor Flores' son. We saw him many times at the store working with his father. He was always very nice," I add, trying to think of a way to stall whatever it is Papá plans to tell me.

"Abuelito heard Máximo was coming through Texas, so he asked him if he'd deliver the letter on his way up to Red Ridge, Oklahoma, to a brewery up there where his cousin can get him a job."

"Please don't be angry with me, Papá!" I plead. "I didn't know what else to do. He asked me to keep the box hidden until you asked for it. He said if I told anyone, it could bring danger to our family. I am sorry for not telling you. I hid it when we got here and haven't looked at it, not once!" Relief and shame wash over me.

Papá's eyes soften. "I am proud of you, *m'ijita*. What you did took great courage. I am sorry you had to bear the burden so long."

"Why is it so dangerous, and why did Abuelito want me to bring it here?"

The warm wind rushes through the trees and dark clouds glide in. I smell the rain that's yet to fall.

"He's had that box hidden in the stable for more than fifty years, and for all that time he's carried an enormous guilt inside him. His letter tells a story that is hard to believe, but he is an honest man and would never lie about something like this. I'm sure he feels better having told his secret."

"What does it say?"

Papá reaches into his back pocket and pulls out the letter.

July 4, 1911

To Adán de León
1918 Washington Street
Seneca, Texas

From David de León
Rancho Encantado
Mariposa, México

Adán, my son,

I got your letter and was relieved to read that you arrived safely. Francisca heard the Ramírez family was not so fortunate. You may remember Jorge. He came to Mariposa from Sandoval a few years ago and worked night and day on the Trujillo farm but could not make enough money even to feed his family. With the revolution moving north and no opportunity here, they left for Texas to join relatives a week after you. The second night they found a place to set up camp and rest, but before they even finished unloading, a pack of wolves came at them lunging at the horses. The horse carrying Señora Ramírez and little Olivia reared up. The poor child was thrown from the horse and trampled when it came down on her. She was only five years old, God rest her soul. Jorge shot and killed two of the wolves and the rest ran off, but it was too late for the child. She died the next day. They brought her back to Mariposa and buried her here. Señora Ramírez speaks to no one but God through prayer. Olivia was their only child to live past the age of three. The other two died from the fever within a few weeks of each other some years back. I know you will pray for the family.

Adán, the real reason I am writing is to tell you about another serious matter. It's been a month since you left Mariposa and there has been no sign of Pancho Villa or his men. The town is quiet. Perhaps they will never come, and it'll turn out it was nothing but a rumor. That is everyone's hope. But if I am being truthful, I believe they will come. The night before you left, I gave a box to Evangelina and made her promise to keep it secret until you received this letter. She does not know its contents. I put her in a difficult position and for that I am sorry. I knew I could trust her to do this important thing for me. If I gave it to you or Maríaelena, you never would have taken it.

Before I tell you about the contents of the box, I must give you the story behind it so you understand how it came to be in my possession.

In the winter of '47 I was nine years old. Comanches raided our town and kidnapped my friend Ernesto Rodríguez as he was tending his herd of sheep and goats. His family and friends searched for months, but he could not be found, and everyone feared he was dead. After a year there were no more searches.

Nine years later a small band of Comanches was seen far outside their own settlement on the outskirts of Correo. We sent scouts to monitor their movement. They came back convinced the Indians were planning an attack. So some of us joined with the citizens of Correo and found the Comanches' camp. We took them by surprise late at night and all but a few were killed.

During the chaos, one of their men caught my eye. His hair was curly, not straight like all the others. He along with a few others escaped into the night.

My memory of this man would not leave me alone after the raid, and a few nights later it came to me in a dream. The curly haired man was Ernesto!

I convinced Ernesto's brother Esteban that Ernesto was alive. We agreed, the two of us would rescue him. We left the next morning and tracked them down. We found their settlement and hid on the outskirts as we watched the day's activity. It didn't take long before we saw him. Ernesto wore buckskin clothes and moccasins and he spoke their language! He wasn't their prisoner. He had become one of them! Still we were determined to get him back.

Ernesto was the first to emerge from his tipi the next morning. What luck! We ambushed him from behind and forcibly took him back to Mariposa with a gun at his back to keep him quiet. He did not want to go!

For a few weeks he hardly spoke. He only spoke Spanish with difficulty. He was distant, not like the boy we all remembered. I stayed with his family the whole time in hopes Ernesto would rediscover his origins, his family and friends.

One night to my surprise he sat at a campfire with me and described how he was abducted and how cruel the Comanches were to him, although his Spanish was broken and heavily accented.

He did women's work for months, had barely anything to eat and was beaten savagely when he cried for his family. Months later he was adopted by an old woman and allowed to learn the language and skills of a Comanche brave—horseback riding, hunting with a bow and arrow and participating in raids on Mexican and American settlers to steal horses and cattle and even kill those who fought back. He learned to love his life as a Comanche and married a Comanche girl.

Ernesto stayed in Mariposa with us for three months but he was unhappy. He seemed ill at ease in his own childhood home. To his family's disappointment, he left to rejoin the tribe.

Weeks before, he had told me a secret that changed my life. If Ernesto knew then what I would do with the information, he never would have told me. The Comanche Chief possessed something of great value, something his people stole from a rich Spanish settler during a raid of his hacienda 100 years earlier.

Ernesto saw it for the first time when he delivered firewood to the chief's tipi the day of the chief's eldest daughter's wedding. He kept his eyes down as he tended the fire but still saw the chief pull out a golden cross covered with jewels from under a buffalo hide. The Comanches believed the cross had powers that could sway the gods in their favor. Ernesto knew the cross would make any man rich. He saw it many more times at ceremonies over the years.

The story of the cross compelled me to do what I have since regretted for many years.

Papá pauses to search my face for a reaction.

"What happened after that?" I probe.

"Abuelito stole the cross."

"I don't believe you . . . not Abuelito. He would never do that," I gasp.

"I am sorry, Evangelina, I wish it weren't true, but it is. The cross would bring enough money for his family to buy more land, lots of land and become part of the wealthy elite in any part of Mexico they chose. It's hard for me to believe it, too, because he is a principled, God-fearing man. But he was young and made a terrible mistake."

"Is there more in the letter?"

"Yes, I'll read you the rest."

I chose my timing carefully. Ernesto said the buffalo migrated across the area every summer. At the first full summer moon the Comanche warriors would hunt for two to three weeks to bring back a whole year's worth of meat, hides, bones, horns and furs. I traveled to the outskirts of the Indian camp on that day and hid while I watched and waited for the men to assemble their hunting party and leave.

Ernesto said the women and children went to the banks of the nearby Río Bravo every morning to get drinking water, bathe and wash clothes. Early the next day I watched them leave camp just as Ernesto said they would. Only a few old men remained. I easily spotted the chief's tipi. Every tipi was plain but this one had hunting scenes painted on all sides—men on horseback with spears, leaping antelope and running buffalo. When the old men and children wandered off, I sneaked to the back of the chief's tipi, slit an opening with my knife and crawled in. I found the cross hidden inside the chief's ceremonial robe, concealed by a stack of animal hides. I dropped it in my boot, mounted my horse and rode away.

I felt exhilarated on the way back home. I imagined all the things I would buy with the money. A farm of my own, a thousand head of cattle and enough supplies to last a lifetime. With that kind of wealth I could have the pick of the most beautiful women in town. Maybe even Adelfa, the most beautiful girl within a hundred miles. But when I got back and had time to think about what I'd done, I grew uneasy. What respectable woman would want to be with me if she knew I'd committed a sin against God? And not just any sin but thievery out of greed and selfishness? Adelfa, the woman I intended to marry was not only beautiful but honorable and kind. She would not have me if she knew what I'd done. I'd been stupid and greedy and wished I could undo it all.

I put my hand on Papá's knee. "So that's what's in the box?"

He nods. "Abuelito went to church every day for weeks, confessed his sins only to God, begged for forgiveness and asked Him what to do, but God was silent—perhaps a punishment for his sin. So he did the only thing he could think of. He put the cross in a box and buried it in the stable where no one would find it. He might have been killed had he tried to return it to the Comanches."

"Why did he make me bring it here, and why was it such a secret? Because he committed a sin?"

"I am afraid not. Rumors swirled for weeks before we left that Pancho Villa was coming to Mariposa to plunder the townspeople for all the riches he could find in order to fund his army and its diminishing supplies. If he wanted something, he'd kill to get it. Of course, no one knew what riches he could possibly want. Even the church had very little that anyone would want to steal. Most people thought it was a hoax and tried to put it out of their minds. But Abuelito thought differently. He wondered if Villa knew about the cross."

"Pancho Villa wants the cross? How could he possibly know Abuelito had it?"

"I'm sure it's nothing more than a rumor. We don't even know if Villa's headed to Mariposa. But your Abuelito didn't want to take any chances. He saw an opportunity to use the cross for a worthy cause. In the letter he instructed me to sell the cross and use the money to improve our lives in Texas, to reclaim the life we lived in Mariposa with land and a home of our own."

"Will you sell it?"

"No." Papá grabs my cold hand in his warm one. "I don't know yet what I'll do. But most Mexicans are far worse off than we are. Many are starving, cannot read or write and have little hope the revolution will give them back even their most basic rights. Maybe that was God's plan for your Abuelito and that cross all along: to help those who cannot help themselves."

"Why did Abuelito give it to me? Why didn't he just give it to you and tell you to sell it in Texas?"

"He knew I would not take it. The cross was stolen, and using it for our own personal gain would be a sin. Greed is an ugly thing, and I am not motivated by money but by what is right. Abuelito figured once we were here, I would bend and use the cross to start again."

"But why me, though? Why not give it to one of the boys?"

"Because he trusted *you*. You remind him of Abuelita. You two have a special bond."

I sit quiet for a minute and think about everything I've heard.

"What if it's not a rumor? Will Pancho Villa go to Mariposa looking for the cross?".

"I've thought of that, too, *m'ija*, but your Abuelito is safe at René's family's house way up on the hillside. No one could find him there. As soon as we hear from Francisca that Tomás is well enough to travel, I will go back. If René hasn't sold the herd by then, I'll sell it, even if I have to take a loss on it. When I get back, we'll move into a place of our own. I suspect we'll be here for a while."

My eyes start to sting, and my insides flutter like the leaves of our orchard trees when the wind picks up. "It will be dangerous, Papá!"

"Not any more dangerous than it was coming here. The job at the brick factory doesn't pay much. I could go farther out and take a job working for the railroad, like your uncle, or in the mines like your brother, but I would be away most of the time. We have the financial means in Mexico . . . I just need to go back and get it. And God willing, bring your brother back here with me."

"Can I go with you?" I plead. "I want to be the first one to see Abuelito safe and Tomás smile again."

"You're talking like I'm leaving in the morning. Let's just hope we hear from Francisca soon."

"Should I bring you the box with the cross in it?" I ask. The secret box is a secret no more.

"You must be anxious to see it after all this time."

My beautiful doll Belinda is lying face down, the hiding space inside her back open and exposed. The cross lies in the box on a stale-smelling cloth, with paper and hay packed around it. Intricate gold etching peeks through the diamonds, rubies, sapphires and emeralds on all four cross-bars. Tiny white pearls form a circle in the middle. Inside the circle, a beautifully painted, haloed Madonna and child look out into the light for the first time in over fifty years.

Chapter Twenty-One
Selim

August 28, 1911

It's my fourth week at this school, and I feel so alone. I understand some of what Mrs. Abbott says in class, but I've said less than ten sentences since I got here, embarrassed by my fumbling and heavily accented English. To make things worse, it's against the rules to speak Spanish. Last week, a boy named Joaquín got caught speaking Spanish to his sister in the schoolyard. His punishment was one stroke of the cane across his backside with a warning that if he got caught again it would be much worse. Some kids laughed about it this morning as they retold the story.

Still, I sit at this desk every day and try to learn.

It's time for lunch. Only three more hours until I can go home. I reach under my desk and grab the bag Mamá made to hold my lunches. She stitched the edges with red yarn and used it to make a happy looking flower on one side. A few weeks ago it was a burlap sack with twenty pounds of rice brought with us across the border. The thought of rice makes the dull pain in my stomach demand, "Pay attention to me!" There's nothing wrong with rice, but it used to be a side dish, not the main dish.

I'm used to fresh eggs, bean and cheese tamales topped with tomatoes and peppers from our garden, bread pudding with apples and even barbecue on special occasions.

In Seneca, we have rice and beans most of the time, or potatoes. Sometimes I bring home sweet, chewy figs picked from a tree in an empty field near Tía Cristina's house. Is that stealing? I tell Mamá a girl named Dolores gives them to me because her family has more than they need.

"What do you have in there today, Evangelina?" Rosemary bends at the waist and pinches the tip of her nose. "Beans again?"

The other kids crane their necks to look and laugh at my lunch. "What kind of disgusting brown garbage is that? How many days in a row have you brought beans? It looks like dog poop! What's the matter, can't you Mexicans afford real food? Isn't that what they feed hogs?"

I can't understand everything she says, but I understand enough to know she's making fun of me. Heat rushes up my neck. I keep my head down and say nothing. If I try to defend myself, it'll only get worse. I can't string enough English words together to make a whole sentence.

Rosemary picks up my bag with the tips of her thumb and forefinger. "What is this made out of, anyway? It looks like a potato sack. It is! It's a potato sack! Who brings a potato sack to school? Probably has bugs crawling in it." She drops it on my desk.

The laughing thunders in my ears. I watch the door, praying for Missus Abbott to come back. Someone, please rescue me.

The door opens. Hallelujah! Missus Abbott must have read my thoughts. Only, it's not Missus Abbott. It's Selim, the very nice-looking older boy who loaned me his chalk-board on the first day of school. I'm thankful for the dis-traction, until I hear Victor throw out insults of his own.

"Hey, camel boy, you know what this is?" He points at my lunch bag with the pretty red flower. "Looks like one of your momma's dresses! Yeah! One of her dresses!"

Victor grabs my bag and throws it at Selim, who catch-es it, glares at Victor and then walks calmly over to my desk. The world goes into slow motion. Dark eyes with long lashes hold mine for what seems like minutes. Where did all the noise go? He crouches down so our faces are level and sets the bag on the desk. I feel his warm breath on me.

"Evangelina, do you want to go outside for a while? I don't think Mrs. Abbott will mind."

I nod my head silently, completely unable to form words—English or Spanish.

Victor is not done with us yet. "Where are you going, camel boy? Back to your own country, I hope! You two deserve each other. This is America! Nobody wants you here, and one of you only talks Mexican. Don't come back here 'til you can talk God's English, you hear me?"

Selim holds out his hand to help me out of my desk. I'm too embarrassed to take it, so I stand up by myself. He's older than me and much taller than I expected. He must be a whole head taller than Papá. I've never been this close to him before, although I do admit I've looked at him many times. Many, many times. He sits on the opposite side of the classroom near the front. I sit in the back and hope Mrs. Abbott forgets I'm there. I bet every girl looks at Selim when they think he's not paying atten-tion. Rosemary stares at him more than all the other girls combined, even though he's a foreigner and she says she hates foreigners. I try not to stare, because it isn't proper, but he's the most wonderful boy I've ever seen. His loopy black curls fall just below his ears and swoop across his forehead. He's got a shadow of a mustache and full lips. I'm looking at a boy's lips!

My breaths come in short choppy waves. I shouldn't be with this boy unaccompanied by a chaperone and, even worse, a boy who's not Mexican! Would Papá be angry if he knew I was out here with a Lebanese boy?

———

We step outside into the blasting sun. I follow him down the stairs and across the road.

"There's a place we can go down here. It's not very far," he says, pointing to a large, flat rock surrounded by knee-high grass and dandelions with white, fluffy tops.

He sits down, grabs my hand and pulls me to sit down too. I quickly fold my hands on my lap. The side of his leg touches the side of mine.

"Evangelina, I'm sorry they teased you. There was no reason for them to treat you like that. I still get teased, and I've been in this country three years. We moved to Seneca only a year ago. Where did your family come from?"

I keep my eyes down. "English no good," I say, embarrassed.

He turns toward me and lifts my chin with his fingertips. Dear Jesus! He's touching my face!

"Don't be ashamed. I understand what you're going through. You're smart. You just need more time to learn the language. It will come, I promise. I can help if you want." His eyes hold mine for a few seconds, then glance away.

I suck in my breath and touch his hand lightly. "Thank you."

His skin is rough, but everything else about him is warm and safe.

Mrs. Abbott calls out. "Selim, Evangelina, no one gave you permission to leave the building! Class is starting! Now!"

"We should go inside," Selim says as he helps me up.

We walk into the classroom, and he runs to his desk and pulls out some bread wrapped in a white cloth. "Here," he says, arm extended. The long muscles in his forearm move in tiny waves. "You never got to eat your lunch. Take this. I'm sorry it's not much."

"Get in your seat, Mister Njaim! You're already in enough trouble with me for taking . . . taking . . . that girl outside," Mrs. Abbott scolds. She still doesn't know my name.

The eyes of every student are on us. Rosemary scowls at me hatefully, but I don't care. I just touched a boy's hand.

Chapter Twenty-Two
Separate the Inferior

November 11, 1911

A steady stream of horses clip clop down the road, their riders on their way somewhere, maybe to work or a restaurant for a cup of coffee or the bank or a store or even home. I've caught myself saying, "I'm going home" or "I left my coat at home" or "When we get home, we'll have to . . . " Tía Cristina and Tío Mario's home is starting to feel like my own home. I guess home is not so much a place, a particular house or city. It's where the people you love are.

I sit under an orange tree in a small park across the street from the school. Our school day routine is predictable. First, we write spelling words and make sentences with them. We learn about American history and lots about the great state of Texas! We've drawn the map of Texas at least ten times and filled in all the big cities.

Missus Abbot never mentions the war in Mexico. I think she should, but I don't say anything. It's not even history; it's happening right now. Stories of the war cover the front page of *The Seneca Herald* with photographs of President Díaz and Francisco Madero and Emiliano Zapata. Madero just won the presidential election, breaking the Díaz dictatorship, but Missus Abbot must not think it's important.

After lunch comes science and arithmatic. We foreigners go downstairs. That means me, Alfonso, Selim, an Irish boy named Patty, a few younger Mexican girls, Beatriz and Anna and two other Mexican boys who just moved here. The Negro sisters Fanny and Jinny left town. One day they were here, and the next day they were gone. Their brother Selby followed an Anglo lady home, trying to sell her some beads his mother made, and went back the next day to try again. The Anglo lady's father came out the front door and shot him like an egg-stealing coyote. I asked Papá one night at dinner about it. He said he hadn't heard anything, but he looked sideways across the room at Mamá when he said it. I barely slept that night. Poor Fanny and Jinny. I wish I could have told them how sorry I was.

Alfonso is the one I talk to most at school. That is, he talks to me the most. That boy can talk! Selim talks to me, too, but he makes me so nervous, I can hardly reply. I mostly smile and nod yes at whatever he says. My English has gotten much better though, so I'm working up the courage to say something to him. He really *looks* at me when he talks, like he's studying me. I wouldn't be surprised if I floated away next time he does that. He brought me a daisy the other day. I pressed it between the pages of my Texas history book, right after we drew the outline of the great state of Texas again and wrote in the state flower (bluebonnet), state tree (pecan) and two famous Texans (Sam Houston and James Polk).

Our afternoon teacher, Missus Clayton, teaches us to say the pledge of allegiance, how to set the table, brush our teeth, wash clothes and other things that "build character." Last week she said, "Your parents' generation is already lost, but by teaching you I can save the next generation of foreigners who come here, uninvited." Or that's what Alfonso said she said. I told this to Mamá.

She responded, "*M'ija*, you are already a person of strong character, and that woman is too stupid to see it."

I never heard Mamá talk like that before.

Mostly I like learning. I look forward to going to school. Of course, I also like Selim, and he's at school, but it's my secret. Not even Elsa knows, and Mamá and Papá would not approve. He's an older boy, plus he's Lebanese. I have to marry a Mexican. But, what if I fall in love with someone from England, or Poland, or Lebanon or even the United States?

It must almost be time for class to start. More children file into the yard out front and run around. Sparse grass covers the ground around the building. A large oak tree stands on one side and a pecan tree on the other. Pecans dot the ground. I cross the road, make my way to the tree, bend down, scoop up some nuts and drop them in my pocket. Mamá will love these for her apple empanadas. We had lots of pecans and walnuts at the rancho. This is only one tree. We must have had thirty.

"Whatcha got there?" a boy shouts from across the yard.

My heart jumps. Does he think I'm stealing? I look up, but he's not talking to me.

"Come here and find out," Rosemary orders. She stands in front of the schoolhouse steps as the flouncy layers of her sunshine yellow dress flutter in the breeze. "It's *very* important business."

Her blonde ponytail forms one solid tube-curl. A white and yellow striped bow clips on each side of her

head. She cups one hand next to her mouth and screech-
es, "Come'n, get one!"

Kids clamor around her and hold out their hands. I
grab another handful of nuts, drop them in my other
pocket, walk towards her and hold out my hand.

"Hah! You don't get one of these," she sneers. "This is
about you, not *for* you, you dummy!"

Hearing what this big mouth has to say is one disad-
vantage of learning English.

Alfonso sneaks up behind her, snatches a paper from
her hand, runs ahead, turns around and sticks his tongue
out at her.

"You filthy animal!" she squawks. "You're nothing but
a dirty, stupid, Mexican. My father is going to kick you
out of this school. You just wait!"

Samantha and Judith quickly rush to Rosemary's side.
Their perfect curls match Rosemary's, as if they planned
it.

"Don't you mind him," Judith soothes.

Samantha puts her arm around Rosemary's shoulder.
"He'll get his due," she assures loudly enough for us to
hear. "Don't they know your father has a lot of say around
here? Let's go. They're not good enough to share the
same air with us."

"Yeah!" Judith jeers. "Go back to Mexico! We don't
want your germs!"

Alfonso glances over the note and hands it to me.
"Look at this," he says. "Can you believe it?"

I try to read it, but give up part way. "You take it. I
can't read all of it. What does it say?"

"Okay, I'll read it to you." He clears his throat. "'Attention . . . something of Seneca.'" His face scrunches up. "I
can't read this word," he says, pointing to the word "citi-

zens" on the note. I don't know what it means either. "'Town Hall Meeting Wednesday Night, 7 o'clock pm," he continues. "'Seneca Courthouse. Topic: Separate the Inferior. No More Mexicans, Negroes or Other Foreigners in Seneca Schools. Join Us for this Important Discussion Led by Frank Silver, Respected Business Owner and Seneca County Council member!'"

"What does it mean?"

I start to chew the nail on my thumb but think again. I want my nails to look nice, if Selim ever looks at my hands. Maybe I'll never bite my nails again.

"Do you really want to know?" Selim answers.

I whip around. He's right behind me.

"Hello," I say shyly. "How is you?"

"Fine, just fine," he answers. "The note says they don't want foreigners in this school. Don't worry about Rosemary. She's just jealous of you."

"Jealous?" I ask Alfonso. "What does that mean?"

"*Celosa*," Alfonso translates.

"Jealous? How come?" I ask, puzzled.

"Because you're so pretty," Selim replies, turns and runs up the school steps.

Chapter Twenty-Three
Fraud

November 13, 1911

Thirty-two bottles, canisters and jars of varying sizes and colors line the shelves next to Doctor Taylor's desk. I counted them, twice. I bring each one down carefully and set them, in order, on the white marble countertop of the little table against the wall. A thin layer of dust covers the shelves, except for the perfectly clean, rectangular and round spaces where the medicines sat. I swipe a cloth across each shelf, dust the bottles one at a time and put them back in their original places. Vapo Cresoline. Anderson's Chill Tonic. Dr. R.H. Jensen's Pin Worm Syrup. McNeil Dyspepsia Bitters. Blood Purifier and Nerve Tonic. Halliday's Cough Balsam. Old Nanny Bickers' Sarsaparilla. Castor's Cure for Gout and Rheumatism. And many more I don't understand. The first week I started working here, when I couldn't even make a sentence in English, I wrote a list for Alfonso so he could tell me what "sarsaparilla," "gout," "rheumatism," "bickers," "purifier" and "balsam" mean. He looked at me like I was asking the dumbest question he ever heard, shrugged and ran off to climb a tree.

There are many other words I don't understand around here. When I hear things like, "chisel," "forceps," "pulsograph" and "pyrometer," I get lost in the conversation. Of course, I'm not part of the conversation, but I do listen. If I'm quiet, Doctor Taylor lets me do my cleaning in the next room over while he talks to a patient, listens to their heart or looks in their ears. I watch for the signal. When he raises his hand, it's time to leave. When no patients are in the room, he shows me the equipment and explains what each thing is used for. I've held a few in my hand. I even looked inside his microscope at a bug's wing. Doctor Taylor says I'm smart.

On the wall above the desk hangs a paper with fancy writing from the school he went to and a photo of him and his wife on their wedding day. He's gone today, off seeing a patient, a retired doctor two towns away, so this is my chance to study the photos.

He looks so young standing in his suit with the flower on his lapel, his hair perfectly parted and slicked down. His bride sits beside him on a small, tufted sofa with a rounded back and wooden legs carved like paws. She leans slightly so her head and shoulder nearly touch his side. A bouquet of flowers rests in her lap. A billowy veil falls softly around her shoulders. I wonder how long it was after this photo was taken that she and their baby died. Her beautiful face with the light eyes and sweet, barely-there smile make my heart ache. All these years later, Doctor Taylor has never remarried.

The doctor helps me with my English and even lets me look at the pictures in his medical books. He doesn't use them anymore, so he lent them to me, to study. I've already memorized the bones in the human skeleton on page eight of *The Everyday Medicine Series*, Volume I.

Now I'm starting on the muscle groups. Doctor Taylor said he'll quiz me in a week. Maybe I'll be a doctor someday. Actually, it was Doctor Taylor's idea. The first Mexican in Seneca to become a doctor! That would make my family so proud, especially Abuelito! And whoever heard of a girl doctor?

"Evangelina, are you there?" Doctor Taylor calls from the top of the stairs.

"Yes, I here." I scurry away from the photos. "I dust your office."

The doctor thumps down the stairs and walks briskly toward me. "It's 'I *am* here,' and 'I *am dusting* your office.'"

"I am dusting your office," I repeat.

"Okay, no more English lessons. Evangelina, you will not believe what I learned today!" He rubs his hands together in excitement.

"What?"

"You know Rosemary's father, Mister Silver, the owner of the Funeral Home, the one who's speaking tonight at the Town Hall?" He looks at his watch. "Less than two hours from now."

"He sick?"

"I'm sure he's fine. But I went to see old Doc Hicks today. Poor Doc's got painful joints and a deep cough. Gave him liniment for his aches and pains and vapor oil for the cough. He can barely catch his breath. Might be more serious than a cough, so I'll check up on him in a week. I bet he wouldn't mind if you came with me. I told him all about you. You could learn a few things."

"Thank you, but what he say about Rosemary's father?"

"Yes, yes. I was getting to that. I was talking to the doctor about the Town Hall meeting tonight and what a bitter, hateful man Frank Silver has become. Some in this town see his money and boastfulness and follow him around like sheep, refusing to think for themselves. Such a shame. Admiring a man with an ego the size of Texas! Anyway, I was complaining about Frank Silver and what a bully he is, and the doctor told me a very interesting story about Mister Silver."

"Tell me!"

"Doctor Hicks' father was a judge in Astor County. Died some thirty years ago. After he passed, Doc Hicks went through all his father's papers and found something, something he kept all this time. He gave it to me today, and I have it right here," he pats his coat pocket.

"What?"

"It's a copy of Frank Silver's birth certificate issued by the local church in Astor City. Only, Frank Silver's name was not Frank Silver when he was born. It was . . . it *is* Francisco Rubén Silva."

"No understand."

"Don't you see?" he pulls the paper out of his pocket and unfolds it. "His mother was Elena Victoria Cruz from Spain, and his father was José María Francisco Silva from Nopales, Mexico. Can you believe it? That man hates anyone with brown skin, spits his venom at anyone different, but he's the son of foreigners himself! Must have changed his name."

"How you know that his birth paper?"

"Frank Silver managed to track it down years ago. Threatened Doc Hicks with closing his business if he told anyone. But Doc Hicks wouldn't give it to him. Filed it away."

"So Rosemary is part Mexican, like me?"

"Yes, and the people of Seneca deserve to know the man with the big opinion is a hypocrite."

"Hypocrite?"

"That man's a fraud. A phony. Someone who pretends to be something other than what he is. When he spouts off his nonsense at the Town Hall tonight, I'll be right behind him to share the news. And you must come."

"I ask my parents," I respond excitedly. I grab my shawl, run up the basement stairs, step outside and hop down the front steps.

Papá sits in Tía's kitchen.

"Please!" I plead.

"Why would I let you go, only to be the subject of that man's hatred?" Papá folds his hands resolutely on top of the kitchen table.

"Papá," I sit in a chair opposite him. "Doctor Taylor got important information today. He's going to share it at the Town Hall, and he wants me there. And, I want to go."

"What information, *m'ija?* What could be so important that Doctor Taylor would want you to hear that man's despicable lies?"

"Señor Silver is the son of foreigners."

"What?" Tía Cristina asks, stunned. She stands in the doorway between the hall and the kitchen.

"Oh, Tía, I didn't see you there!" I exclaim. "I'm sorry if I woke you."

"No, I was already awake. I came to get Leticia some pineapple juice. We're reading a book in my bedroom. Tito is sleeping. What did you say about Frank Silver?"

"His given name is Francisco Silva. His father was from Nopales, and his mother was from Spain. He only calls himself Frank Silver."

"Did you say Frank Silver is part Mexican?" Mamá walks in from the living room.

"Yes, that's what I said," I beam. "Doctor Taylor has his birth paper to prove it."

"I'm going with you to that meeting." Mamá steps away and returns with a coat around her shoulders. "I met that man once," she says to Papá. "He was heartless and arrogant."

"I'm coming, too," Tía adds. "My children deserve to get an education like any other child in this town. We are all God's children. A church-going man like him should know that."

"Are you feeling up to it?" my mother questions.

It's only been the past month that Tía has been showing signs of her old self, singing to Leticia, smiling at the baby, making meals.

"I will be there to support Doctor Taylor," she responds confidently. "He's been good to me. And my children will get an education, right here in Seneca. Mario can watch the little ones."

Chapter Twenty-Four
Love Thy Neighbor

November 13, 1911

Mamá, Papá, Tía and I stand at the back of the crowded courtroom, which I've seen many times, but never with this many people in it, especially women!

Now that I'm here I can take a good look around. A long rectangular table with carved legs and five stiff-looking tall-backed chairs face a podium in the front center of the room. A similar looking table and wooden chairs with U-shaped backs sit on a raised platform against the side wall, also pointed toward the podium so jurors can see everyone. A fancy gold-framed portrait of the Texas Governor, Oscar Branch Colquitt, hangs behind the front table on a dark paneled wall. Another portrait of President William H. Taft hangs behind the jurors' table. An American flag drapes from a flagpole in the left front corner of the room. Flags are so much prettier when they flutter in the breeze. I like the American flag with all the stars, but the Mexican flag is more interesting. What other flag has an eagle with a snake in its mouth?

There must be thirty rows of tightly packed chairs. Some people I recognize from the shops around town, but many I don't. A few rows up from us, three men in sombreros and cowboy boots clump together against the wall. The man with the unlit cigar hanging from his lips works at the *carnicería* where Tía buys her meat. I don't recognize the other two men.

The man with the cigar approaches Papá. "Good evening, friends!"

"*¡Buenas noches,* Guillermo!" Papá responds.

"What do you think will happen here tonight?" Guillermo asks.

"We'll see, but this effort to keep our children out of school is groundless and ridiculous." Papá announces.

"I have three kids at home who should attend school. I'm here for them," Guillermo explains. "My friends have children, too. Their wives made them come."

He nods toward his companions who walk up to Papá, shake his hand and introduce themselves as Armando Peña and Esteban Castañeda.

The tortilla baker at the market on Washington Street stands just beyond them. Many Anglo customers shop there because everything's cheaper there than in town. She speaks at least some English, because when she's not making tortillas, she's finding things for Anglo ladies or helping them pay up front, sometimes with money and sometimes with goods from home, like eggs, milk, butter, sausages or boxes of fruit and vegetables. A young boy sits cross-legged on the floor and runs a wooden train back and forth in front of her.

In the public seating area Anglo ladies in full skirts and high-neck blouses swish their lacey fans to circulate the air, thick with cigar smoke, men's cologne and dinner smells on people's clothes. Some hold squirming toddlers or sleeping babies, and a few shush their older children.

Most of the men wear jeans, button-up shirts and cowboy boots, but a few wear suits and bowties.

Missus Abbot and Missus Clayton chat busily in the first row, their mouths a blur of motion. Old Mister Greer from the Post Office sits next to them. The family from the yellow house across from the entrance to Washington Street sits toward the back, near us. I've seen the man tending the yard. He looks asleep, but he can't fool me. His eyes open a sliver as he sizes up his family, then closes his eyes again and pretends to snore softly. The woman fusses over the children. All but the smallest one go to my school.

"Evangelina!" Doctor Taylor, calls, as he snakes his way through the crowd and grabs my outstretched hand with both of his. "So glad you came."

"Thank you," I reply. "I scared."

"Don't be! You have as much right to be here as everyone else. I'm glad to see your parents here."

He removes his hat and bows to my mother and aunt. "Hello, Mister and Missus de León and Missus Benavides. I am glad to see all of you."

My father shakes the doctor's hand. "Hello, Doctor. We here to . . . "

"Russell! How very good of you to come!" Judge O'Leary butts in and extends a plump hand to Doctor Taylor.

I've seen him before, but always in his fancy robe. He's the one who swatted Alfonso with the "Board of Education" for speaking Spanish at school.

"A well-respected man in this community such as yourself should have his voice heard," the Judge tells him. "Make sure to speak up when ole windbag Silver takes a breath!" He says, slapping Doctor Taylor on the back. "But why are you back here with these people?" The judge throws up his hands. "Don't they know what we'll be talkin' about? Of course not!" he snorts. "They can't read or write!" he says, looking sideways at Papá.

"Good evening, Your Honor," Papá states clearly in English and extends his hand.

The judge knits his eyebrows, mutters under his breath and looks away. His puffy jowls and round cheeks remind me of bread dough that's risen too long.

"Well, naturally, I believe in equal treatment under the law. That's what I stan' for, as ya know," he boasts. "But these here people cross the border like waves of rats pourin' outta floodin' basement. Then they want food and a place to build their nests. Then," he leans in, "they think they actually belong here! The good-standin' reputation of this community is at risk, Russell. Now c'mon up front with me."

"Thank you, Your Honor," Doctor Taylor replies, tipping his hat. "But as you well know, some of 'these people,' as you call them, are descendants of Mexican families who owned ranches in and around Seneca, long before any of us arrived. These are friends of mine, and I'm fortunate to have their fine company this evening."

Red splotches appear on the judge's neck folds. "I don't know what's gotten inta ya." He pokes his finger in Doctor Taylor's chest. "Maybe you're not feelin' well. That must be it, 'cause if I din't know better, I'd say you sound ill. Now you stop talkin' nonsense afore you dig yourself inta a hole you can't crawl outta. Now, if you'll 'scuse me, the man of the hour jus' walked in."

A low rumble of a hundred hushed conversations sweeps through the crowd. People twist their necks to see Frank Silver and his family come through the door.

Rosemary struts past me.

"Ahem," I clear my throat.

She stops, drops her mother's hand, whips around and looks me up and down with a sneer.

"Hola, Rosemary. How are you tonight?" I gush.

"What are *you* doing here?" she snorts. "My God, you're even stupider than I thought you were. Don't you get it? Nobody wants you here."

"Thank you," I respond with extra honey in my voice. "It's so nice to see you, too, Rosemary."

She pivots with a toss of her hair and rejoins her family, swaggering regally down the middle aisle of the courtroom. The "man of the hour" shakes hands and waves at the crowd.

"Hello everyone! Thank you for comin'!" he crows.

Missus Silver extends her pale arm for dainty handshakes and a few pecks on the top of her petite hand. Rosemary's brother, Frankie, runs ahead and flops on the ground cross-legged in the very front. Mother and daughter take their seats, cross their ankles and fuss with their dresses until they lay in perfect folds.

Frank Silver steps behind the podium. Frankie scoots closer and watches his father like a dog eager for a bone.

"Good evenin', my fellow Senecans!" he starts.

Behind him a line of staunch looking, stiff-backed men sit in their stiff-backed chairs behind the long formal table. Judge O'Leary is among them.

"My distinguished fellow council members and I," he says, gesturing toward the grim-faced men at the table, "can't tell you how pleased we are to see you here. Your attendance demonstrates you care about this community as much as we do."

"That's right!" a short stout man in a cowboy hat at the back of the room yells. "Those filthy foreigners are takin' over our town and the good railroad jobs!"

"Now hold on there, Samson," Frank Silver insists. "Let's review the facts 'fore we go judgin' anyone. As a city councilmember and business owner, I base my opinions on fact, not gut feelins."

The audience bobs their puppet heads in approval.

"Awright, les' hear dem facts!" Samson shouts.

"Well the question before us tonight is, should we allow the children of Mexicans and Negroes and Chinamen to attend the same school as our own precious young?"

"No!" half the room hollers.

"Hell no!" a man adds.

Missus Abbot stands up and says, "If they don't speak English, I can't hardly teach 'em!"

"For that matter," Frank Silver continues, "should we allow children of any foreigners inta our schools?" He cocks his head and squints as if deep in thought. "We've been mighty generous so far. That's why we've got the Mexicans, the Irish, the Italians, the Jews, the Polish, the Lebanese and God knows what else taking over our town . . . and towns like ours all over the great state of Texas . . . and Arizona and California and New Mexico, too. Now, I've been readin' the newspapers and even talked with a professor at the college over in Alden. He's been studyin' these issues and shared some very interesting facts with me. But first, let me start by sayin' the obvious. Mexicans are a mongrel race. That's a fact you can't argue with. Not even you Samson!" Laughter erupts.

"They've already banned 'em from the school in Loma," Samson jeers. "Towns all over Texas are doin' the same thing, and California, too! An' after we ban 'em from the school, we should do it for the theater, public parks and restaurants! This *was* an upstandin' town 'fore they showed up!"

I tighten my throat and shut my eyes tight to keep the tears back.

"Awright, Samson. Let's just stick to the topic at hand, shall we? Where was I? Oh yes . . . " Frank Silver taps his chin. "The mongrel Mexican race. To be more accurate," he prattles on, "they've been adulterated by centuries of intermarriage between the Spaniards and the inferior Indian race. This has produced a third, inferior, mixed race. Mixed breeds are feebleminded and incapable of making a living in a civilized society. Anglos, on the other hand, are the descendants of Adam and Eve, God's chosen people."

He pulls a paper out of his pocket, unfolds it, puts on his spectacles and scans the page. "Professor Schmidt's studies prove that Mexicans and other foreign students have eighty five percent of the IQs the Anglo students do and some even less."

"Schoolin' 'em wit' our own chillen is a waste a money!" a bald man in front insists.

"And it holds our own chillen back!" another man pumps his fist in the air.

"I couldn't agree more, gentlemen," Frank Silver replies. "And . . . ," he starts, pointing a fat finger at the ceiling to make his next point, "foreign culture is backwards. We've witnessed it ourselves. The men come here, unskilled and unable to learn a real trade. The women just have more babies, addin' to the problem!"

"Make dem sinners go back to wherever dey came from!" shouts a woman holding a toddler on her hip.

"I could go on and on, but I think this is a good time to pause and hear what *you* all have to say. My intention is not to monopolize the conversation."

People crane their necks and look around in hopes someone else will speak up.

"Y'all came here for a reason," Frank Silver says. "A democracy requires discussion, even opposin' opinions. Whaddya wanta say?"

"I have something," Doctor Taylor volunteers.

"Thank you for getting us started, Doc."

Just then, Judge O'Leary shoves his chair back, scrambles over to Frank Silver and whispers something in his ear. Frank Silver scratches his cheek and swallows. The lump in his throat bobs up and down.

The judge stomps back to his seat, plunks down and whispers furiously to the other men.

"I have here," Doctor Taylor declares, "a piece of a paper." He holds up the birth certificate. "A true fact rather than emotional outbursts."

"Is that right? What does that paper have to do with the discussion here tonight?" Frank Silver challenges.

"I'll get to that. But before I do, let me say this clearly. Your so-called facts are total rubbish, Frank."

"Hold on there!" Samson stands up and growls.

"That's a city councilman you're talkin' to!" the long-faced councilman next to Judge O'Leary reprimands the doctor.

"Frank, I don't care what that professor says," Doctor Taylor scolds. "Do you know why the foreign born students scored lower on the IQ tests? Because the tests were administered in English to students who hadn't had time yet to learn the language. How well would you score if you were given an IQ test written in German?"

"But this is the United States of America and the language here is the King's English," Frank Silver scoffs.

"All right, but let me ask you this, Frank. What language did your own father speak? Was it the King's English? And what about your mother?"

A tangle of voices lift up and fill the air. Even the sleepy man from the yellow house sits up and prattles at his wife.

"What?" Frank Silver sputters. "What're you getting at?" His eyes dart between his wife and the councilmen who sit forward in their seats. "I never even knew my father. He died when I was a babe in arms." He wipes the back of his neck with a handkerchief.

"Your father was Mexican, Frank. And your mother was from Spain."

"That's a bald-faced lie!" Frank Silver yowls.

"Lie?"

Doctor Taylor steps behind the podium and forces Frank Silver to step back. "I'll counter your bald-faced lies with a real fact. This," the doctor holds up the paper defiantly, "is your birth certificate, Frank. But your name's not Frank, is it?"

I bite my lip. Mamá squeezes Papá's arm. Their mouths hang open. Tía Cristina grins.

"Your real name is Francisco Rubén Silva. Your father, José María Francisco Silva, was born in Mexico. Your mother, Elena Cruz, was born in the north of Spain."

God, please forgive me, but despite my usual desperate need for peace and predictability, I can't wait to see where this goes.

"According to your own initiative, Frank," Doctor Taylor goes on, "as the child of a Mexican father and Spanish mother, your own children are of foreign parentage and would not be admitted to this town's only school! Is that what you want?"

"Frank Silver does not speak for me!" a pregnant woman stands up and shouts defiantly.

The man next to her grips her dress sleeve and yanks her back down. "Sit down, Amy!" the man orders his wife.

"Frank Silver does not speak for me either! Did Moses not, through the word of God, lead the Israelites out of Egypt?" says a young man in dark pants, suspenders and a striped cap. "Do we presume to play the role of God when we say who can and cannot live among us?"

"Thank you, Missus Harris and Mister Sutherland," Doctor Taylor says.

He looks over people's heads toward the back of the courtroom. "Evangelina," he says, "will you come up here? These people should meet someone who'd be denied an education because of this backward proposal."

I search my parents' faces in a panic. Tía frantically translates for them.

"Go on, he's calling for you." Papá turns me forward by the shoulders and points to the podium.

"Evangelina is fourteen years old," Doctor Taylor announces, waving me forward.

"Why is *she* going up there?" Rosemary asks her mother loud enough for everyone to hear.

"Don't let that Mexican go up there!" Missus Silver screams. "Who is she to address these good Christian people?"

Old Mister Greer from the lumber store pats her hand. "Come on now, Joanna. Let the good doctor talk. After all, it sounds like your own husband is one of them mongrels he talked about."

"Shut your mouth!" Missus Silver shrieks.

"Evangelina," Doctor Taylor continues, "is the same age as my daughter would have been, had she survived childbirth. My wife, Susanna, and baby girl, Evelyn Rose, died fourteen years ago, God rest their souls. Evelyn would have lived a privileged life here and had every opportunity open to her, but it was not in the Lord's plan. Now, why should this young lady be any different? Because she was born two hundred miles away? Because she speaks a language native to her country? She came to Texas with her family to escape the revolution. If your own family was in danger of being murdered, would you stay and wait for it to happen? Would you knowingly leave your loved ones in harm's way?"

Tía Cristina walks forward, smiles at the crowd confidently, moves to my side and wraps her arm around my waist. "Lift your head up," she urges me. "Show them you are proud of who you are."

I lift my head up and see Rosemary bore into me with her snake eyes.

"I've known many of you for years," Doctor Taylor says to the crowd. "Heck! I delivered some of you myself! You're good people with big hearts! Do you think foreigners love their families any less than you do? Do you think it was easy to leave their homes and risk their lives for the privilege of living in this town?"

Frank Silver backs up slowly as if no one's watching and slinks away quietly along the wall. Rosemary, her brother and mother tiptoe down the aisle they paraded in like peacocks twenty minutes ago. Missus Silver extends her arms around Rosemary and Frankie in a semi-circle to shield them from the watchful crowd as they disappear through the exit door. Four families, including the one from the yellow house, Missus Abbot, Missus Clayton, two white-haired women and the man named Samson follow them.

"You should be ashamed of yourself, doctor!" one of the elderly women in a patchwork bonnet hisses as she makes her way out.

"I appreciate your patience with me folks," he says, smiling at the captivated crowd. "Just a few more points, and I'll wrap up, I promise.

"Some of the people Mister Silver criticizes were highly respected and well-educated in their own language and country. Others were uneducated, simple, hardworking folks, anxious to start again without the fear of starving, being robbed, kidnapped or murdered. Just because you had the good fortune of being born in this country makes you no smarter, more deserving or more civilized than someone born elsewhere.

"On that subject, didn't your family hail from Ireland, Judge O'Leary? If your family had not been allowed into this country or you'd been denied an education, where would you be today?"

"Don't compare me to those illiterates!" the judge sputters.

"I want to introduce you to this young woman," Doctor Taylor says, ignoring the judge. "Whatever happens, I'm going to ensure she gets a proper education, but I expect this community to provide her and all children the education they deserve."

"Doctor?" I tug on his sleeve as politely as I can.

"Yes?" He tilts his head. "Evangelina, do you have something to say?"

My parents signal the three men in sombreros and the woman from the *mercado* and her son to move forward. All seven hurry forward and stand next to my tía.

"Yes, sir. Thank you. I . . . I . . . want to learn at school, and thank you for all you teach me, but . . . " I look out across the rows and rows of faces. "Did God not say, 'Love thy neighbor as yourself,' and 'Let us not love in word, neither in tongue, but in deed and in truth?'"

Some people stare at me, astonished. Some smile, and others whisper to each other or move restlessly in their chairs.

"You are right young lady, that is what the good Lord said," Mister Greer pipes up. He places both hands on his cane, pushes to a stand and sets his hat on his head. "I wish you and your family every success here, Evangelina. Despite all of Frank Silver's bluster, the people of Seneca believe in the Lord's teachings, and they'll find it in their hearts to live His word. Now, I'm not in charge, but I do believe this meeting is over, unless anyone else has something to add?"

People stand up and gather their things.

"I didn't think so," he continues. "Everything we needed to know has already been said."

Mister Greer gradually makes his way down the aisle, and others file in behind.

"I have not dismissed the meeting yet!" Judge O'Leary rails.

A tall thin man in a dark suit and bow tie steps from behind the table, puts his arm around the judge's shoulder and leads him back toward the other council members. Together, they move as one to a door at the front of the room and file out.

Chapter Twenty-Five
The Enemy of Triumph

November 13, 1911

We approach the house and jabber non-stop about what just happened. I don't know if I've ever felt this good. I wish Abuelito could have seen me up there! He always said, "Fear is the enemy of triumph," and he was right! I was brave tonight, for once. There was no predictable outcome, and it was a wonderful surprise ending!

"The doctor is a hero in my mind, as well as you, my dear," Tía says, beaming. "You were so brave!"

I hug Tía's arm and bounce up the walkway. "I'm ashamed to admit this, but I can hardly wait to see the look on Rosemary's face at school tomorrow!"

Papá pulls open the door. "After you, ladies." He bows and ushers us in.

"Hello!" I call out cheerfully. "Tío?"

I wish Elsa was home so I could share it with her, too. She got a job at Lady Wright's Boutique and Alterations last week and usually stays late.

"What's going on?" Tío Mario emerges from his room with Tito squirming and fussing in one arm and Leticia holding his free hand.

"Mamá!" Leticia runs to her mother.

"Hello, sweet girl," Tía says, crouching down to kiss her cheek. "It was quite an evening, Mario," she announces. "We'll be talking about this for a long time to come! Let me see if I can get them both down for the night, and I'll join you when I can."

She walks down the hall with Leticia trailing behind her. The bedroom door closes with a click.

"Where's Domingo?" Mamá asks.

"He fell asleep on our bed," Tío says, gesturing toward the room.

"*M'ija*, tell Tío about the meeting," Mamá says as Papá slides her coat off her shoulders.

"Have a seat, and I'll go get us something to drink," Mamá offers. "You go ahead. I'll be back in a moment."

"Tío, you should have heard Doctor Taylor!" I begin. "And Frank Silver! Doctor Taylor made him look so foolish! He said . . . I mean Frank Silver said, not Doctor Taylor . . . he said we're part of an inferior race and we're not as smart at the Anglos! Can you believe it? And . . . "

"Hold on a minute, Evangelina." Tío holds up his hand. "Slow down. Why don't you start at the beginning? First, you got to the courthouse. Then someone started the meeting. Was it Frank Silver?"

Mamá brings glasses and a pitcher of hibiscus tea. Tío pulls a bottle of tequila out of a cupboard in the living room and pours two shot glasses, one for him and one for Papá. Mamá goes and gets her own shot glass.

We settle in the living room.

"We had a remarkable experience at the Town Hall meeting tonight," Papá begins. "It started with Frank Silver filling people's ears with complete nonsense . . . that we're less intelligent, carry diseases and have low moral standards! The whole meeting was to get people on his side, to bar our children from getting an education."

"Low moral standards?" Tío Mario repeats indignantly. "That bigot wouldn't bury my stillborn son!" He tips his shot glass and swallows the tequila in one gulp.

"He's a hypocrite," Papá scoffs. "Doctor Taylor got him, though, when he produced his birth certificate. His real name's Francisco Silva! He's half Mexican and half Spanish himself! His proposal to adopt that irrational, ignorant law would bar his own daughter and son from school.

"A toast! To Evangelina, to Doctor Taylor, to equality!" Papá announces, glass high in the air.

Glasses clink. Such a happy sound.

November 14, 1911

I sit up on the floor in a tangled heap of blankets. Elsa and Domingo breathe slow, regular, rumbly sleeping breaths. They've gotten used to sleeping on the hard floor. But me, I can't wait to sleep on a real bed again!

"That's wonderful, Maríaelena!" Tía cries from down the hall.

I stand up, put on my housedress and scurry to the kitchen.

"What's going on?" I ask.

"We got a letter from your sister this morning," Mamá explains. "God has answered our prayers! Your brother is better!" Mamá grabs my arm and squeezes. "Isn't it wonderful?"

"Unless there's an objection, I'll catch a train tomorrow morning. I don't want to wait," Papá proposes. "I'll have to sell our last rifle to get the money for a ticket, but so be it."

"Thank God!" I clap my hands together. "Did she say anything more about Tomás?"

"Just that he's gotten stronger and is eating like a little piglet again." Mamá grins and hands me her handkerchief.

I wipe my nose. "And Abuelito? Did she say anything about Abuelito?"

"He's had a bit of a cough that he just can't shake, but otherwise, he's fine," she assures me. "René sold half the herd. It was the best he could do, and perhaps it's best they didn't sell them all. If we go back, the remaining cattle will be there for us to start again."

"If." She said, "if."

"I'll leave the cross with the Iglesia de la Paz, Church of Peace, as we discussed," Papá adds. "Father Roberto will be more than surprised."

Chapter Twenty-Six

Mariposa Wings

December 4, 1911

I'm early as usual and pass the time under my favorite orange tree picking long-stemmed clovers and tying them into a ring. My fifteenth birthday is six months away, so I resist the urge to put it on my head like a crown and pretend I'm a princess. Growing up means having less fun. At least, I think it does. I'll have to ask Elsa, since she's already fifteen and a half.

The sun emerges from behind a cloud. I lift my face to the sky, close my eyes and feel the warmth soak into my face and body.

"Can I sit with you?" The creamy light glistens behind Selim's dark silhouette.

"Oh, I did not see you come," I exclaim. "You can sit." I pat the grass beside me.

He plunks down and settles in cross-legged. He smells of soap and something vaguely earthy and sweet. Ahhh, I close my eyes and take it in. Does he always smell this good?

"Evangelina?"

"I sorry! You say something?" Stop smelling him and start listening to him!

"Um, yes. I said I haven't been to school lately. You might have noticed." His curly black hair pops out from under an old, scuffed up cowboy hat.

"Yes, I notice." I say, nonchalantly imagining how his hair would feel if I ran my fingers through it.

"I was working at the mill. They lost three of their men to railroad jobs. I came here to tell you . . . to let you know . . . I won't be coming to school anymore."

Please, no!

"I've been coming here for almost two years, and there isn't much more for me to learn. The savings we brought with us is gone. To be honest, I've only been coming the past few months to see you."

I clamp my jaw and hold my breath so my chin won't wobble.

"Evangelina?" He shifts his body, so we're face to face.

"Yes?"

"I want to keeping seeing you. Do you understand? I want to know you better."

My insides feel wiggly and strange and wonderful, but my tongue is paralyzed.

"So, what do you say?"

Phew! He rescued me from having to come up with something.

"Can we . . . spend more time together? I want us to be close. Do you understand what I'm asking?"

"Yes," I whisper.

He lays his warm hand on top of my cool one.

The school bell rings abruptly. The sounds of noisy children fill the air. Where did *they* come from?

"When will I see you?" he asks.

"I do not know," is all I can manage. My brain is nothing but mush!

"I will come here every school day at eleven o'clock until I get regular work. Meet me across the street at the flat rock where we went on your first day here." He points across the road. "We'll have lunch together."

"Yes, I be there," I reply.

"Okay, I'll see you tomorrow." He lifts the clover crown gingerly and places it on my head. "I pronounce you my 'Princess Evangelina.'" He lightly kisses the top of my hand and runs off. His long strides carry him farther and farther until he disappears into the horizon.

———

Rosemary does her best to ignore me, which is fine, because at least she doesn't go out of her way to be rude like before. After all, she and everyone else knows she's part Mexican, so it's possible we're related! Wouldn't that be funny?

"Hi, cousin!" I said to her as we passed in class the day after the Town Hall meeting.

She stared straight ahead and stomped off. That's all I ever said about it. I could have teased her more. That's what she would have done to me, if it were the other way around, but that's not the kind of person my parents raised. But sometimes, on the inside and only on the inside, I gloat. I revel in the memory of that Town Hall meeting, my friendship with Doctor Taylor and my brief moment of bravery. I can't be a good Catholic girl every moment of every day, can I?

Missus Abbott won't look in my direction, even when I raise my hand. I work hard and learn, despite her. But today, I admit, is an exception. I cannot stop thinking about Selim and what might be. What might be. What might be. I like the sound of that. I imagine his hand on mine. I imagine him squeezing my hand and touching my cheek. I imagine his full lips on mine. ¡Híjole! Is it right to dream about something . . . something, so, forbidden? What would my parents think of my friendship with a Lebanese boy? In Mexico, it would be a definite "no." In Mexico, even *I* wouldn't have considered it. But here, to my own surprise, I'm considering it. I'm more than considering it. I want it more than words can say.

I don't go to Missus Clayton's class in the afternoon anymore. After the Town Hall meeting, no one showed up, so they canceled the Americanization Program. I'm grateful I no longer have to listen to her teach me how to become "a neat and efficient house servant or skilled manual laborer."

Doctor Taylor's medical practice is my afternoon class now, three days a week. More foreigners come to his office than before, some even from the next town over. I interpret for the Spanish speakers, and Doctor Taylor pays me an extra dollar, although plenty of patients don't pay him with money. They give him things, including a top hat, a saddle, chickens, bales of hay for Tillie, firewood, loaves of bread, eggs, spices, jugs of honey, bolts of fabric and other odds and ends. One man paid him with a bottle of expensive whiskey. The doctor trades some of it to the Seneca General Store and gets cash in return. Everything else he uses.

Today, I sweep, mop, dust and fold laundry. I like helping around the doctor's house. Besides, his mother can't do much herself after falling and breaking her wrist. At first she barked orders at me and slammed doors when I was around, but now, we talk a little. Bringing her *pan de dulce* or *biscochitos* helps. Last Saturday I made a special trip to take her meatball soup with zucchini, corn, tomatoes, potatoes and a rich, spiced broth. Good food softens hearts, Abuelito always says.

With the housecleaning done and Doctor Taylor on a house call, I head home for Domingo's birthday dinner.

The family sits at the kitchen table, moved just for tonight into the living room to celebrate Domingo's fifth birthday. White candles glow on each side of one of Tía's painted vases filled with cheerful geranium flowers.

"The *arroz con pollo* was delicious, Tía," Enrique says, patting his stomach, "but I ate too much of it."

"I hope you have room for praline candy," Tía says over her shoulder as she steps into the kitchen. "Your Mamá made it, so you know it's good."

"Oh," Enrique groans, "I suppose I can make room for just one, or maybe two, possibly three."

Tía, Elsa and I clear the dishes away. Mamá picks up the platter with the candy and carries it to the living room. We trail behind her and launch into the birthday song.

Estas son, las mañanitas, que cantaba el Rey David,
a las muchachas bonitas, se las cantamos a ti.
Despierta mi bien, despierta, mira que ya amaneció.
Ya los pajarillos cantan, la luna ya se metió.
Qué linda está . . .

"¡*Feliz cumpleaños, Domingo!* Happy Birthday, Domingo!" Papá and Tomás shout from the kitchen. They must have snuck in the back door!

"Mamá!" Tomás runs to Mamá and throws his arms around her. "I missed you!" He rubs his face back and forth in her hair.

"Oh, I missed you so much, m'ijo. I don't ever want us to be apart again, ever. Thank God, you are well. Let me look at you." Tears stream down her face.

She sets him down, kneels, puts her hands on his shoulders and looks him over. "You're so thin, my little one! Do you feel all right?"

"Yes, Mamá. I can't run or I get out of breath. But the doctor said I'll be able to run fast as lightning again someday. See?" His boney knees pump up and down as he runs in place. "Is that candy?" he squeals, pointing to the platter on the table.

"Here, m'ijo," Tía says, passing the platter to him. "You probably don't remember me. I'm your tía Cristina, and this is your tío Mario. What a sweet angel face you have! We're so glad you made it here safely."

"Tomás! Tomás! Come here!" I nearly shout. "I can't wait another second!"

"See, Evangelina, see? I'm okay now!" He turns in a circle and bites into his sweet treat, sending candy crumbs all over the floor. "Francisca took good care of me."

"Thank the Lord!" Mamá exclaims.

Enrique rumples Tomás' hair. "How is Abuelito?"

"He is fine, but not the rancho." Tomás frowns at Papá.

Mamá's smile evaporates. "Adán? What does he mean?"

"I was going to tell you later. Maybe I should wait until after dessert?" he suggests.

"Adán, tell me now."

Papá squeezes his eyes shut and takes a deep breath before he begins. "It was quite a shock when I arrived. They set the place on fire, and there was almost nothing left. The house, the barn, all of it, and they took the remaining cattle and goats, all the animals except Álvaro. He was with Francisca and René." Papá runs his fingers across his forehead, his gaze unfocused and distant.

"What?!" My brain reels. "That can't be!" I put my hand over my eyes. Our home! We were supposed to go back home!

"Who did it? The *villistas*?" Enrique asks.

"Yes, *m'ijo*, a week before I arrived, soldiers tore the town apart just as we feared. And it wasn't just Mariposa. The neighboring towns suffered the same fate. When Pancho Villa runs out of money, he funds his army by robbing trains, stealing livestock and ransacking every town he crosses. That man is destroying Mexico at the same time that he's trying to save it."

"What about the rest of the family? Please say they're safe!" Elsa implores.

"René's mother passed away even before the *villistas* came through, God rest her soul . . . but we knew it was coming. Francisca, René and the rest of his family are all well."

I tap Papá on the shoulder softly. "And Abuelito?"

"He is . . . " he pauses, " . . . your Abuelito is safe. He's had a terrible cough for over a month. Francisca sent word to Doctor Gonzales to stop by and check on him. Your abuelito's slowing down, but he is seventy-three years old. It was extremely hard leaving him, but he sends his love and prayers and asked us all not to worry about him."

"What about the rest of the town?" Mamá asks.

"I'm afraid Rodrigo's mother, Isabel Treviño, was shot and killed. The little ones hid in the cellar and survived. Pedro and Martín were off bidding on farm equipment.

Rodrigo was at his grandmother's repairing damage from a windstorm. He's the one who found Isabel."

Mamá sighs. "Oh, what a shame. That poor woman. What a cruel irony that she lost her life at the hands of the same men who kidnapped her husband and son."

"What happened?" Elsa asks, bewildered. "I thought they would leave Mariposa, like we did. Rodrigo's father is the one who told us the soldiers were coming."

"They did leave, but in six months, Villa never came, and they had a farm to get back to," Papá explains. "They had only been back a few weeks."

"What a terrible shock it must have been," Elsa murmurs.

"They're doing their best to cope with the situation. Isabel's sister is a widow and lives alone less than a day's travel from here. Pedro asked that I share the bad news with her and ask for her help with his children. I'll go tomorrow. If she agrees, Rodrigo will stay at her house and look for work. Martín will stay and help his father rebuild the farm."

"Poor Rodrigo, finding his mother like that." Elsa places her hand over her chest. "When will he arrive?"

"I don't know for sure, m'ija, but I spoke with him before we left. He's anxious to see you, and I'm sure you'll bring him great comfort. He asked for permission to court you, and I happily gave him my blessing."

Tears roll down Elsa's face in a steady stream. I put my arm around her waist.

"Adán," Mamá says, "just think what might have happened if any of us had stayed at the ranch. We should give thanks to the Lord."

We hold hands in a circle around the table and bow our heads low. The candles flicker and cast moving shadows on the wall like the uneasy souls of the departed.

"Thank you for blessing our lives," Papá begins. "You shower us with abundant blessings of grace, peace and love and we are forever grateful. Please keep our minds pure, despite the treachery and sins of others, as we strive to see the good in all things. Let our actions reflect your word, so that when doubt and grief overwhelm us, faith will inspire us to work once more for the good of others and always for Your glory. In Jesus' name, amen."

"Papá, tell us about the cross," Enrique says.

"The *villistas* stormed the church and took everything that wasn't nailed down. Father Roberto was more than grateful for the cross. I didn't tell him where it came from, only that it would be impossible to return it to its original owners. The Comanches are long gone from northern Mexico. The cross will be sold, most likely in Mexico City, and used to replace what was stolen and help Mariposa rebuild what was lost. But with the current dangers, it could be months or even years. No one will be traveling to Mexico City anytime soon.

"Oh, and, Evangelina, before I forget," Papá continues. "Abuelito asked me to give you this note." He pulls an envelope from his pocket.

Everyone's gone to bed. The stillness of the house makes it too easy to think and feel. I'm numb. Well, not numb. Angry. Lost. Confused. Relieved?

What is wrong with me? This is shameful! How can I feel relieved if I love Mariposa? I've been trying to predict how my life will go since before Elsa's *quinceañera*. Will I live out my life in Mariposa, where I have all the answers? Or will I stay here and fight for things I never even thought of before? Dreams I didn't know were possible. My world was small and comforting back then. My world is big now and full of prospects. If I study and continue with school, I could become a nurse, or a doctor even. Selim isn't a dream, and he's more than a possibility. He wants to be with me, and as hard as it's going to be—a Lebanese boy and a Mexican girl—I want to be with him. I feel it. We're supposed to be with each other.

Six months ago my answer would have been as certain as the crickets' song on a summer night. My life was in Mexico, on the ranch. Now, the revolution grows, Mexico's future is uncertain, Mariposa is in shambles and the ranch is gone.

Challenges are chances in disguise, Abuelito says.

I open the screen door gradually, hoping it won't creak. I sit on the front step with one of Tía's sweaters wrapped tightly around me. The full moon that shines on me, shines on Abuelito, too, providing all the light I need to read his letter.

21 November

My dearest Evangelina, your father tells me you are doing well in school and even getting lessons from the local doctor. That is wonderful news! I always knew you were smart like your Abuelito. He also said you spoke bravely in front of a large crowd at a town meeting. I couldn't be more proud! M'ija, what your father told me just confirms what I've known all along, that you would blossom from a loving curious child into a confident, compassionate, determined young lady capable of doing anything you set your mind to.

The reason I am writing is that you came to me in a dream the night after you left, and I felt I must tell you about it. You stood at the river's edge peacefully watching the waters of the Río Bravo rush past. Dark clouds rolled in and opened up from the heavens, releasing a great rainstorm. You lifted your face to the sky and let it hit your skin and soak your clothes. Suddenly a lone wolf appeared beside you and drank from the river with a stunning butterfly perched on its shoulder! It lifted and flew around you in a spiral again and again, but you did not cry out or move. You simply waved it south toward the Sierra Madre and the warm waters of the Gulf. I could not put the dream out of my mind, m'ija. Then I remembered a story I told you many, many years ago about how our little town got its name. Do you remember?

When you were born, it was a blessing from God, a sign of His goodness and grace, like the butterflies. God wants you to dream just like the mariposas *did. Then spread your wings, and go get your dream.*

Love,
Abuelito

I look at the vast and sparkling sky, stretch my arms out and imagine myself lifting off this earthly ground.